They Don't Have Horses
on the Moon

They Don't Have Horses on the Moon

Daisylands

Raoul Hawkins

They Don't Have Horses on the Moon
Daisylands

iUniverse books may be ordered through booksellers or by contacting:

iUniverse
1663 Liberty Drive
Bloomington, IN 47403
www.iuniverse.com
1-800-Authors (1-800-288-4677)

Because of the dynamic nature of the Internet, any web addresses or links contained in this book may have changed since publication and may no longer be valid. The views expressed in this work are solely those of the author and do not necessarily reflect the views of the publisher, and the publisher hereby disclaims any responsibility for them.

Any people depicted in stock imagery provided by Thinkstock are models, and such images are being used for illustrative purposes only.
Certain stock imagery © Thinkstock.

ISBN: 978-1-4759-9228-1 (sc)
ISBN: 978-1-4759-9229-8 (e)

Library of Congress Control Number: 2013910830

Print information available on the last page.

iUniverse rev. date: 03/08/2018

Contents

Introduction

MALT DAISY WAS A SELF-MADE man, a fact he reminded the world of at every opportunity. Of modest stature, with a trim moustache and pleasant smile, he had power and influence far beyond his temporal limits, having perceived early in his career a great and eternal truth through which he touched the lives of all his fellow country folk.

"The way to a parent's wallet is through the demands of his or her offspring."

He used this insight to forge a mighty empire, the center of which was Daisylands, an elaborate amusement park and affiliated film studio that captivated, enthralled, and entertained successive generations. His cartoon characters "Mickey Moose" and "Donald Goose" became icons of American culture, winning the hearts of the children and shaping the consciousness of subsequent generations.

Malt himself was a paradoxical character, a strange blend of sweet and sour. Pampered by a doting mother who fussed over her "little Daisy" and brutalized by his father, a dance hall musician who practiced relentlessly and unmercifully on the bass saxophone, Malt was a man who searched religiously for perfect harmony, beauty, and large amounts of money, no matter how ugly he had to get to achieve them. From humble origins to vast excess—an expression of the American dream, coated in glucose and dished up with every serving of apple pie—his name was chiseled into American legend beside Andrew Carnegie and John Dodge.

But the more you have, the more you have to lose, and Malter Daisy had plenty. At the end of his life, he threw down his challenge to mortality in a desperate attempt to keep his kingdom, and had his cancer-riddled body frozen in a cryogenic hibernation capsule. Like a twentieth-century mummy, the emperor was preserved until the day he could be revived and cured to live again—and build new empires. But Malt was to discover another eternal truth. Human biochemistry has an unstoppable momentum and its own destiny to fulfill.

1

Daisylands

MALT DAISY HAD BEEN DEAD for thirty-nine years. The second millennium had dawned, and with it came a new era of civilization, an era in which Daisylands was to feature more prominently than anybody present at the park's fiftieth anniversary celebration could know.

Daisylands was more than just an amusement park; it brought together the most contemporary innovations in the arts, the sciences, technology, and marketing, and tied them into a complete package that could be physically experienced by everybody who enjoyed spectacular rides, themed worlds, and fantastic creations. It had opened amidst much fanfare in 1955, and the tumult was repeated for its semicentenary, an occasion marking not only fifty years of glorious history, but one that heralded a rebirth of the Daisy empire. Malter Daisy Jr., grandson and heir to the Daisy Dynasty, had taken control of the family company as its president and chairman of the board. His opening address in this capacity was to be made at the Anniversary Day Parade for the semicentenary celebration, and representatives from every national media organization were in attendance. One such organization was the *Los Angeles Tribune*, which had sent its star reporter to cover the event.

Neil Hamilton was an upwardly mobile, young Californian professional of average height, average weight, and average intelligence (for a star reporter). He didn't want to be covering this story and was purposefully loitering beneath the stage from which Malter Daisy Jr. was speaking, when it collapsed on top of him. One moment he was bored beyond belief and the next he found himself lying in a hospital bed. In just a few more moments, he would be sore, dazed, and thoroughly confused, but being bored was to become a thing of the past.

The doctor arrived. He swept into the room in the manner of an extraterrestrial beaming in from the mother craft. A sly smugness licked the lips of his baby face and dangled invisibly from his upturned nose.

"Ah, Mr. Hamilton," he announced confidently as he strode to the side of the bed, his swelled chest riding high on his ample frame.

"Doctor?" the reporter queried lamely. The white coat and officious clipboard were dead giveaways.

"Dr. Barnyard, the president's personal physician," he boasted while punching a combination into a panel of buttons on the wall. A screen appeared above the bed board and displayed a series of graphs that confirmed the patient was suffering from a cardiac condition, diabetes, an inflamed liver, kidney malfunction, mild emphysema and the early stages of leukemia. In all other respects, he appeared to be in good health.

"Hmm," the doctor mused. "That seems fine. You'll be out of here by nightfall."

Neil, who could not see the screen discernibly from where he lay and who would never know all the details it proclaimed, was instantly relieved.

"Yes." The doctor laughed. "Three more days in a coma and you would have been food parcels for the wastelands."

His bewildered patient didn't quite see the humor of this remark but managed a few meek chuckles in reciprocation.

"Where am I? What happened?" he ventured.

"Touch of amnesia, eh?" Dr. Barnyard probed. "Yes, not so surprising. You were in a bit of a pile-up at the parade on Sunday. Three days ago now. Almost lost Governor Van Drake, we did. Put everybody in the same ambulance and brought you straight here. Best private clinic in the world, you know. We resuscitated the president in this very building."

"Resuscitated!" Neil echoed. "Was he sick?"

"Sick! He was dead. Suspended in animation. Cryogenics. You know, put on ice. Your amnesia must be worse than I thought." The doctor looked concerned, but he shrugged it off and informed his patient that his wife would be notified and could collect him that evening. The reporter thanked him before he left, but the doctor insisted he had done nothing.

"All we can do with comatosis is wait," he said, and then he was gone.

Neil felt disoriented, and his head hurt. On top of this, his bodily functions demanded their natural relief, and with this urgency in mind, he hopped out of bed and wandered into the hall and down the corridor. Unable to find any sign that indicated a men's room, he opened the nearest door.

No urinal or washbasin was in sight; this was just another wardroom. Its only occupant, an old man with short grey hair and a thin moustache, was sitting in a wheelchair and staring, as if in a trance, at a portrait of Mickey Moose hanging on the wall. His meditations interrupted, the old man turned to Neil but said nothing. He looked familiar though his face bore no exceptional features beyond his whiskers.

"I need to find a bathroom," Neil said, breaking the silence.

"What happened to your head?" the old man questioned in reply. Neil could feel the bandage on the side of his head.

"A stage fell on me," he said quickly, fighting the impulse to double over and cross his legs.

"A stage fell on you!" the old man laughed. "*Ha*, you're not the first person to be stage-struck." He laughed again, guffawing and slapping his thigh. "Stage-struck!" he repeated.

"Well," the man said when he'd recomposed himself. "You sure as hell picked the best place to get stage-struck in. Look at me. I came in for a heart job, and they've already replaced my knee caps." He motioned towards the bandages that peeked out from under his nightshirt. "Yes, *siree*. Ain't nothin' they can't fix these days."

"Comatosis," Neil interjected.

"What?" the old man blustered, his pale complexion flushing.

"They can't fix comatosis. All they can do is wait," Neil replied, gnashing his teeth.

"What's comatosis? Well, it doesn't matter anyway. They can fix everything else. Why I've had every organ in my body replaced. I feel better now than I did before I died."

Must be in the psychiatric ward, Neil thought, his bladder near bursting.

"I really do need to get to the bathroom," he pleaded.

"Over there." The older man pointed, and Neil was through the self-closing door so fast, it was as if he'd never been there at all.

But emptying his bladder, all three days' worth, was to be his last moment of contentment. Though he wasn't what would be described a "health freak", like many young upwardly mobile Californian professionals, he liked to stay in shape. He worked out at the gym at least once a week and played tennis religiously every Saturday morning with his wife, Helen, and a group of like-minded yuppies from the office. He had even competed in one or two public fun runs, events he had at least managed to complete. His diet was adequate, overseen by his wife, who was a vegetarian and suspicious of any food that wasn't a good, earthy color. She only bought brown rice or raw sugar and always did her shopping in the morning, "when the energy was better." Although it could not have been said he was particularly handsome, and in fact, it never had been, except by some doting aunts when he was very young, he had high cheek bones, a refined snout for a nose and his hazel eyes shone with a healthy lustre. He was, in short, a reasonable interpretation of a male Homo sapien in his late twenties, or so he thought. But the face that gazed in disbelief at him from the mirror above the washbasin mocked this impression.

Mortified, Neil was overcome with an all-consuming paralysis. Even his breathing stopped. The face in the mirror was pallid, its skin pitted, and its hair, a faded shade of his usual jet-black, thinning and struggling to make an impact above the bandage circling his forehead. Ashen stubble covered its chin and gaunt cheeks, and cloudy eyes stared dimly through a fog that rivaled the pea soupers of nineteenth century London. Was this the face of Neil Hamilton?

Neil had aged at least ten years, and not even graciously. He took a step back; then he moved closer to the mirror to scrutinize his features; then he stepped back again. He slapped himself several times across his face and shook his head violently from right to left, but the image in the mirror wouldn't change. Overcome with despair, he screamed, dropped to the floor, and pounded it with his fist until his distress was superseded by an objective embarrassment that caused him to sit up and pull himself together.

He must have been there for a very long time, though he was not really aware of time passing. No one disturbed him. He strained to remember what had happened before he blacked out and awoke in his wardroom, but his mind remained a blank. He recalled Barnyard saying he had only been unconscious for three days, but he'd heard of people who'd been in comas for years and then suddenly jumped up one morning and asked for a bowl of muesli. With a grim resolve to learn the truth, he splashed

4

some water on his craggy new face and prepared to reenter the world. He wanted some answers.

Neil's long absence had gone totally unnoticed by his benefactor in the adjoining room. The old man's attention had been arrested by another visitor who arrived almost the moment the bathroom door closed behind the hapless reporter. Boyish despite his advanced years, radiating youth and vitality from the loose folds of a green tracksuit and peaked cap, this diminutive newcomer held rank and position far beyond that suggested by his attire. He was in fact, the secretary of state of the United States, Jimmy to his friends, and senior member of "the Club." He had come to see the old man in his wheelchair on important federal business, for the old man was none other than the president of the United States.

A national crisis was brewing. The entire South American continent had been discovered to be cultivating and processing an exotic new drug, which drug lords were selling to their northern neighbors. In a multi-billion dollar operation, Latin America was seen to be growing fat as America decayed from within. It had to stop. This was the message the secretary brought to his president, and he had several papers, measures designed to bring the traffic to a halt, prepared for his signature. The old man was so incensed at these revelations, his heart threatened to collapse before he reached surgery.

"We need to impose this blockade straight away," the secretary insisted, his hard blue eyes popping to convey urgency. "Military intervention will have to be discussed at the next meeting of the Club."

"Do you want me to sign these things now?" the old man asked.

"It is important," the secretary replied.

"What's the matter? Afraid I won't make it through the operation?" The old man's confidence in the doctors belied a natural terror of the operating theater.

"Don't be silly," the secretary jeered, snarling from one corner of his lopsided mouth. "It's just that it's urgent. The situation is criminal. It's an offense against America, God, and Mickey Moose."

Desecrating the name of Mickey Moose was a sacrilege that could not be tolerated. The old man was duly reverent.

"What do I have to sign then?" he sighed with resignation.

"Jesus!" the secretary exclaimed.

"Isn't Malt sufficient?" the old man seemed surprised.

"Jesus!" Jimmy gasped again. "Who's he?"

5

The bathroom door had just popped open to reveal the perplexed and defeated-looking figure of Neil in a patient's gown.

"How'd he get in here?" Jimmy demanded.

"Oh, the fella with the big bladder." The old man swiveled his chair around to face his visitor.

"How's it goin', young fella?" he asked cheerily, the distraction coming as a welcome escape from pressing affairs of state.

"Young!" Neil screamed involuntarily.

"What's he doing here?" the secretary raged. "He looks like an outsider."

"He was looking for a toilet," the president explained. "Even outsiders have to piss."

"He shouldn't be here," the secretary lectured. "He could be working for anybody."

"Young!" Neil shrieked again. Both men stared at him.

"Barnard!" Jimmy bellowed then, pointing at Neil, commanded, "Come here!"

Neil shuffled into the room and stood by the wheelchair, glaring incomprehensibly at some point in the air between the two men.

"What's your name, boy?" Jimmy asked officiously.

"Boy!" Neil shouted. He couldn't help himself. The words sprang from his mouth as if by reflex.

"Jesus, this one's right out of funnyland," Jimmy quipped.

"Take it easy on him," the old man urged. "He's probably had a brain transplant or something."

"Easy!" Jimmy's pale face flushed hot pink. "We're about to go to war, and you say take it easy? He could be a spy."

He frisked Neil quickly for any large objects that may have been concealed in his gown, but he couldn't find any.

"He looks harmless," he eventually conceded, resting his hands on his hips. "What ward did you come from, soldier?"

"Ward!" Neil echoed as the hall door flew open and Dr. Barnyard marched in with his usual air of bravado.

"Ah, doctor," the old man greeted him.

"Barnyard!" Neil yelled. It seemed to be the word that triggered him into animation. "I'm old. I'm ugly. I'm old and ugly."

He stumbled a few meek steps towards the doctor and dropped to his knees.

"I've slept my life away. Why didn't you wake me? Why didn't you tell me? Why? Why?" And he began to sob pathetically.

"Jesus, who is this guy?" Jimmy fumed impatiently.

"This is Mr. Hamilton. He was hurt in the Celebrations Day tragedy," Barnyard answered.

"I wanna be young again!" Neil cried at the top of his voice. Jumping to his feet, he rushed to the old man's wheelchair and knelt beside it.

"Feel this," he said. Grabbing the old man's hand, he scrapped the finely boned fingers across his own creased and pitted cheek. "Sandpaper. Old sandpaper. I used to be young."

"Yes, we all used to be," the old man said.

"My eyes, my eyes." Neil leaned over and stuck his eyeball, parted wide by his fingers, against the old man's.

"Look!" he pleaded. "It's a swamp in there!"

The president cringed further into his corner.

"Now, now Mr. Hamilton," Barnyard said as he placed his hands firmly on the irate patient's shoulders and drew him away from the wheelchair. "There's no need to fret. You look fine for a man pushing thirty."

Neil collapsed at the doctor's feet.

"Save me," he grovelled. "Give me a new everything. I'll never sleep again, I promise."

Barnyard smiled uncomfortably at Jimmy and the president.

"It's time for your surgery, Mr. President," he advised, unsure of how to react to the hysterics of the man who clutched his leg.

"President," Neil echoed faintly.

Jimmy punched the air with his fist full of documents.

"You can't go now," he yelled, hurrying to the other side of the old man's chair. "These papers have to be signed."

Barnyard protested.

"But the doctors are waiting."

"Screw the doctors," Jimmy said.

The old man gripped the arm of his chair, clawing at his chest with his other hand.

"Do what you want with them." He grimaced. "But do it after the operation."

Barnyard freed himself from Neil's embrace and took control of the wheelchair from behind.

"I'm afraid we can't wait," he said curtly, driving it through the door. "Wait here Mr. Hamilton," he called, speeding down the hall, with the secretary of state in hot pursuit.

Already anxious and confused about his physical deterioration, Neil now had a new dilemma with which to be reconciled.

"President?" he repeated incredulously, as he recalled the doctor saying he had resuscitated him in that very hospital. Glancing around the room, in search for some clue to the old man's identity, his eyes were drawn to an open briefcase on a desk by the medicine cabinet. Reaching in, he gathered up the paper folder that lay inside. But the sudden appearance of a nurse left him no time to examine it, and with the guilty haste of a snoop caught reading someone's private mail, he stuffed the incriminating papers up the baggy sleeve of his gown. Managing to keep them concealed until he was back in bed, he discretely hid them under the mattress. By that point, there was no need to consult them, as the nurse told him what he wanted to know. He had indeed had an audience with the president of the United States, Malt Daisy.

Neil was speechless. The current president was of such little stature, he couldn't remember his name at any time, but he was sure it wasn't Malt Daisy. He was however, in for ruder shocks. That evening, the woman who greeted him as her husband was not his wife. She felt like Helen, as she hugged him, but she didn't look like Helen. Though when he thought about it, he couldn't remember what Helen did look like.

And then there was his car, which looked as though it had received considerably more wear than he remembered having given it.

"I didn't know there were any of those old gas guzzlers left," the garage attendant said glibly, passing Helen the keys.

As they spilled into the California twilight from the depths of the parking lot, Neil turned in his seat and gazed back at the monolith from which they had emerged. An enormous synthetic crystal of slate, black glass, and concrete, it cleaved its way skyward to a pinnacle floating above the clouds. It was a structure of such colossal size, he couldn't understand how he'd never noticed it before.

"Sure glad we made it out before nightfall," Helen barked over the roar of the wind rushing past. "We wouldn't have wanted to get locked in overnight."

Neil said nothing, retreating to a catatonic state from which he didn't emerge till they reached their destination. On the fifty-seventh floor, in one of a forest of high-rise apartments, Helen and her husband had a squat, one-bedroom flat, a far cry from the suburban bungalow Neil thought he was going home to. He stood on the balcony, built for one, and gazed at the galaxy of lights twinkling into the distance. It was a dazzling display, shaming the stars above which, as if humbled into hiding, were nowhere to be seen.

Dizzied by the ocean of humanity in which he was suspended, he stepped back inside the sterile apartment, which was cluttered with molded plastic furnishings, and stared at the woman who called herself Helen, with her dark hair and darker green eyes, and her face, lean and leathery, looking much older than her twenty-six years.

"Where the hell am I, and who the hell are you?" he exploded, unable to contain his dissatisfaction with these unfamiliar surroundings. Helen looked shocked by his words, then hurt, and finally accepting of the situation.

"They said you'd be delirious," she said, as if this observation was meant to console him. Neil was not consoled.

"I don't understand," he said, glancing around the room, noting the billboard style advertising that substituted for wall art, and the shiny, puce-colored scheme. "I don't remember any of this."

"That's what happens with amnesia," Helen explained patiently.

"But I do remember," Neil said. "It's just that I remember it all differently."

"What's different?" Helen glanced around the room herself. "Nothing ever changes around here."

Neil thought of the face that had gaped at him from the mirror and was visibly distressed.

"Look," his wife said in an attempt to calm him. "Just tell me what you do remember." She put her arm around his shoulders and gave him a squeeze.

"Yes," he said, closing his eyes and breathing deeply. "I'm Neil Hamilton. My parents are Noel and Nellie. They ran a shop in my home town of Springville, Ohio." He cocked an eye at Helen, who nodded with acknowledgement, and continued. "I was born on the tenth of October, seventy-eight, I'm a Libra. I drive a pink VW convertible and still vote republican!"

Haunted by the image in the mirror, he again dropped to the floor and pounded it with his fist. Helen moved to comfort him, but he stood and pushed her back.

"You don't understand," he told her. "I live in a free-standing, weatherboard house in Los Angeles. I've got a good job with the *Tribune*. I've never even been to Daisylands till last week." He stopped and felt compelled to ask the inevitable question.

"And when did Malt Daisy get elected president? He died years ago."

Helen was staring at him, her eyes fearful. "Malt Daisy has been president for ten years," she replied delicately.

Overwhelmed, Neil collapsed into a molded plastic armchair. His whole world, what he could remember of it, had been distorted beyond recognition. Unable to reconcile his memories with his situation, he retired early, in the hope that, by morning, all would be back to normal, whatever that was.

2

The Gangle Was Heading
for the Bedroom

THE EFFECTIVENESS OF THE STREET lighting abated as the first rays of morning sun squeezed between the jigsaw of tenements. Already the early risers were streaming from their skyscrapers in a bid to beat rush hour as a sleek, four-door sedan glided to a halt outside Neil's building with a hiss of hydraulics. A tangle of arms and legs emerged, straightening to become a tall and gangly young man who promptly tripped on the curb and fell in a sprawling mass on the pavement. He dusted himself off, limbs flailing, and rushed into the lobby to hail an elevator. It arrived, its complement bursting uncontrollably from their confinement and trampling the unsuspecting newcomer in the subsequent stampede. He dusted himself off again, only to trip as he alighted on the fifty-seventh floor and stumble into a garbage receptacle that lay in ambush by the door.

Falling over was not an uncommon occurrence for this man, though he did seem to be having an unusually bad morning, even by his standards. He had been highly excitable as a youngster and his twenty-four years had so far produced little mellowing. But today he was especially excited. His lively grey eyes blazed, and his wavy brown hair bounced on his angular, animated face. Today his partner and good friend, Neil, had not only returned from the hospital with all the same parts he went in with, but also this was the day he would have his first ride in a space zoot. Making his way to Neil's apartment, he pounded the door mercilessly until Helen opened it.

"Mornin'," he greeted and pushed his way inside.

"Harvey!" Helen wasn't used to receiving visitors quite so early.

"Well, where is the old bastard?" the visitor asked.

"Harvey, it's six o'clock," Helen scolded.

"I know." Harvey apologized. "I'm running late, but that doesn't mean I don't have time for a coffee." He strode to the galley and punched his order into the café-bar. It delivered its promise in seconds, and he turned back to Helen, who was collecting discarded items of clothing from the floor.

"Well, if he's alive, get him. We've got work to do," he said.

"Harvey, he's very tired; he's still recovering. Come back later." She wanted to go back to sleep herself.

"No way, Helen. We've got a Zoot to catch in an hour. This is the big one, the one we've been waiting for. We can't be late. Go on, get him up." He was insistent, but Helen had inherited all her mother's stubbornness, and her mother could be very stubborn.

"No, Harvey," she said. "Tell Mr. El Duce to assign someone else."

"Helen," Harvey replied, "we've been working on this assignment all year. If you let him sleep through today, he'll never forgive you. Go wake him up."

"You don't understand. He's not feeling himself," she protested. "He's . . ."

The gangle was heading for the bedroom.

"Harvey, no!" She chased him to the door, but he was already inside and clambering on the bed. Neil was shocked and leapt from beneath the covers as if he'd just discovered something small and furry crawling over his body.

"Oh hell!" he exclaimed.

"Hey, that's the way." Harvey laughed, relieved to see his old friend so nimble. Helen hastened to her husband's side and draped a robe over his shoulders. He gathered it around his naked body and gaped at the stranger who scrambled off the bed.

"Hey, old buddy, you came back to us," the stranger said and put forward his hand. Neil was unresponsive, so the stranger squeezed his friend's cheeks till his mouth puckered and gave his head, now free of its bandage, a vigorous shake. "You look great. You look better than you did before the accident.

"Doesn't he look great, Helen?" he said to her and then turned back to Neil. "And she said you weren't feeling well."

He paused for a moment and looked into his friend's vacant eyes.

"Hey, we've got a Zoot to catch; let's move."

Neil didn't move, but he looked instead to Helen for an explanation. "Do you know this guy?" he asked.

"Know me!" Harvey gushed. "What is this?"

He seized Neil by the shoulder and gestured to himself with his other hand.

"It's me, your old pal, Harvey."

"I told you, Harvey," Helen interjected. "He's not feeling himself. Just give him some space."

She dragged her husband into the lounge room and sat him in a plastic armchair.

"I'll get you some coffee," she said and hurried to the auto-kitchen as Harvey stumbled into the room after them.

"But we've got a Zoot to catch!" he protested lamely, seating himself in a second chair. Helen returned with a cup and handed it to her husband who sipped on it quietly.

"Well?" the impatient and bewildered visitor asked.

"Well!" Neil replied slowly, his eyes sinking malevolently into their sockets. "I'd like to know just who you think you are and what the hell you think you're doing here at this hour of the day?"

It was amazing what a cup of coffee could do to pull a man together in the morning.

"Neil," Helen cooed soothingly, "you must remember Harvey. He's been your cameraperson for two years now."

"Remember?" Harvey repeated.

"Cameraperson!" Neil exploded. "I'm a newspaper journalist. I don't work with a cameraperson."

"Newspapers!" Harvey was equally indignant. "Newspapers went out at the turn of the century. Hell, nobody can even read anymore. What are you talking about?"

He turned to Helen.

"What's he talking about?" he asked her.

"You may as well know," she told him. "Neil seems to be having a little trouble with his memory."

"My memory's fine," Neil said firmly. Then after some consideration, he added, "Sort of."

Harvey looked forlornly at Helen and then back to his partner.

"You can't tell me you've forgotten whom we're meant to interview today?" he said.

Neil just gazed at him with a blankness that convinced the cameraperson Neil was not entirely with them, though he had long suspected this anyway.

"The story?" Harvey ventured timidly. Neil remained unimpressed.

"What story?" he asked flatly.

Flabbergasted, Harvey's eyes implored Helen for assistance, but she just shrugged her shoulders as if to say, *What did I tell you*?

"Jesus," he fumed. "The story, the goddamn story. We've only been working on it for the last six months. It's your baby. You did all the research—the company's history from its beginnings as a movie studio to an economic conglomerate that monopolizes the whole goddamn country. What story! Where are your notes, that stuff on the president? How his grandson took a waning amusement park and built it up till it encompassed a continent? What do you think you were doing at Daisylands on Sunday anyway?"

"Sunday?" Neil paused. "I was covering the semicentenary of the parks opening."

Harvey and Helen exchanged concerned glances. The park was one hundred years old, not fifty, but before they could correct him, their silent communion was interrupted by the buzz of the videophone. It erupted to life, engulfing an entire wall, as if another room had just been connected, to reveal a short, fat, rather swarthy-looking individual standing behind the chaos of his desk.

"Hamilton!" he barked, his beady eyes zeroing in on the two men. "I expected to find you ready by now." His tone demanded an explanation.

"Mr. Impiombartu!" Neil responded, surprised to see an image on the wall talking to him but more surprised to realize he knew this person. It was his editor from the *Tribune*.

"Mr. Impiombartu!" Harvey echoed, jumping to attention.

"Shut up, Fisk," the image commanded. "What on God's dirty brown earth do you think you're playing at Hamilton?" He glowered at Neil.

"Lazing around in your goddamn, stinkin' 'I'm inside, you're out,' mod-con, super-spaced, luxury hospital while we're trying to get out a news disc."

"Ah, er, I," Neil stammered.

"Can the crap!" the image persisted. "You've got less than an hour to make the morning zoot to Spacelands. I don't have to tell you how important this story is. It's the first one he's done since Daisy Sr. became president. Don't screw it up!"

"No, I . . ." Neil was becoming emotional. "Mr. Impiombartu, it's you, it's really you." He made a half-hearted attempt to place his cup on the coffee table but missed. It clattered to the floor, spilling its thick, black brew and soaking his robe, which dropped simultaneously as he shuffled several meek steps toward the screen. The image recoiled in distaste as Neil advanced.

"Look you disgusting excuse for a newsperson," it bellowed. "Save me your puerile wit and get your ass in gear or I'll send the boys from public relations over to break every bone in your body."

"Yes, Mr. Impiombartu," Neil blubbered, more from habit than acknowledgment. "Right away. The news, yes."

Harvey relaxed and wiped the gathering beads of perspiration from his brow.

"Well don't just stand there," the image screamed. "Move!"

"Yes, Mr. Impiombartu, move." Neil made a confused effort to go in several directions at once, finally choosing one and walking into Harvey, who having contracted Neil's panic, was attempting to move in several directions himself. Neither managed to get very far, but much energy was expended in trying.

"And Hamilton," the boss's voice added dryly. The two men ceased their frenzy and turned their attention to the video.

"Put some clothes on." The screen went blank and then disappeared, leaving the men alone but for Helen, who covered her face in her hands and leaned abjectly against the wall.

The two reporters looked at each other.

"Well don't just stand there," Neil shouted, filled with a new sense of mission. "Let's move."

Harvey let out a wild, cowboy's yell, and Helen rolled her eyes to the ceiling as Neil dressed and chased his partner down the hall and into the lift. Like a thousand generations before him, Neil's identity was inextricably bound to what he did for a living, the craft upon which rested his survival. Neil was a newsperson. In a world he could find no connection with, this was one thing to which he could relate. Not knowing where he was going didn't matter; he was going somewhere, and that was enough. Journalism flowed in his veins like blood, and once he smelled the trail of a hot story, nothing else mattered. It was his escape from the pressing dilemmas of the world in which he found himself, and from this he drew some comfort.

3

Space Zoot

As MILE UPON MILE OF Brazilian-style shantytowns flashed past the tinted windows of Harvey's Magnobile, Neil reflected glumly on his situation. It was not until his colleague cautiously drew his attention to the fact that Daisylands had just celebrated its one-hundredth year that he suddenly realized where he was. He was in Los Angeles, where he'd always been, but the year was 2055, which explained the strange new surroundings but not how he came to be there. Though still dazed and confused, essential elements were piecing themselves together. Neil had woken in a hospital that specialized in freezing people fifty years after he had entered it. The conclusion seemed obvious.

"How long have we been working together?" Neil asked, hoping to glean something about the new life he deduced he must have.

"Do you even know me at all?" Harvey was shocked and offended.

"Wouldn't know you from a bar of soap." This denial gave Neil a deep satisfaction, as if he could neutralize Harvey's existence by not recognizing it.

"Do the words, 'Malter Daisy III', mean anything to you?" Harvey asked, eyebrows arched. Neil thought for a moment, unable to see any relevance.

"And who is Malter Daisy III?" he asked blandly.

Harvey, aware Neil was unwell, explained with patient trepidation.

"Malter Daisy III," he said, speaking slowly, "is Malter Daisy's grandson."

There was a short and pregnant silence as Neil digested this intelligence.

"What the!" he exploded. "Of course he's his grandson. So what?"

17

He stopped, as if hit by a thunderbolt, and then suddenly burst out laughing. Harvey failed to see the joke, but Neil had just learned he was living in the year 2055, and the ridiculous proposition that Malt Daisy had been resuscitated and elected president of the United States rang with new resonance. He couldn't contain himself. He laughed so hard, tears of mirth streaked his cheeks and splashed on the dashboard.

"When you've finished," his partner in journalism sighed.

"Wait." Neil chortled. "You're going to tell me Malt Daisy is president of the United States."

Harvey shook his head.

"Well isn't he?" he said in disbelief. Neil's body convulsed so violently his head hit the dashboard, denting the interior but not his humor. Harvey simmered quietly, feigning patience as he waited for Neil to pull himself together.

"Want to let me in on the joke?" he asked, barely masking his irritation.

"Oh nothing," Neil mused, regaining his composure. "You know, I had lunch with him yesterday."

Harvey was at a loss for a response, convinced by now that Neil was totally insane.

"You had lunch with him?" he said skeptically.

"Well, I didn't actually have lunch with him," Neil said. "I was wandering around the hospital and went into his room by accident."

"Malt Daisy's?" Harvey queried.

"Yes."

"And he was just standing there?"

"Sitting actually. He'd had his knee caps removed or something."

Harvey's jaw dropped involuntarily.

"Well, what did he say?" he demanded.

Neil shrugged. "He told me where the john was."

The gangly reporter blinked with disbelief and then exploded with rage.

"You had an audience with President Daisy, who's harder to see than Garvey's Ghost and all you got out of him were directions to the john!" He screamed. "And you call yourself a newsperson?"

Neil squirmed in his seat.

"We've been slaving all year on a history of the Daisy Empire," Harvey continued, his voice rising with his blood pressure. "At every stage, we've been denied access to the very man who got the whole thing going over a hundred years ago, and you walk into his room and ask him where the john is?"

Neil was beginning to feel decidedly foolish, the journalist in him recognizing a golden opportunity lost.

"Well what was I meant to ask him?" he said defensively.

"Ask him!" Harvey gasped. "There are a million questions we could have asked him. How does it feel to be dead for nearly a hundred years? Does he like being president? Did his grandmother make good chicken soup for Christ's sake—what do you think we'd ask him?"

Neil was ashamed, his professionalism was compromised, but it was suddenly bolstered as he remembered the documents he'd taken from the president's briefcase. He'd stuffed them into his pocket before leaving the hospital to avoid their detection, and he gladly produced them for his partner.

Harvey was immediately interested and punched a combination into a small keyboard mounted on the dash. Then, taking his eyes off the road altogether, he took the folder and began to browse through it.

"Hey watch where you're going," Neil cried.

"Don't worry," Harvey mumbled dismissively, "these Magnobiles drive themselves." He continued browsing, his eyeballs popping from their sockets as he turned from one page to the next.

"Mickey Moose!" he exclaimed under his breath.

"Well?" Neil queried. Harvey looked at him, his eyes blazing with controlled excitement.

"You really did see the president," he acknowledged.

"Yeah, that's what I said," Neil affirmed smugly while breathing a silent sigh of relief. "So is this stuff hot or what?"

"You stole it, didn't you?" Harvey smirked.

"Come on, come on; what's it say?"

Harvey gazed at his partner and shook his head.

"You mean you haven't looked at this yet?" he said.

Neil smiled sheepishly.

"You've been out all week, you haven't heard," Harvey said, finding excuses for him.

"Heard what?" Neil replied. The suspense was killing him.

"The big bust. South America is growing and selling drugs to service their national debt."

Neil scoffed.

"So what's new?"

Harvey dismissed Neil's indifference to the scale of the problem.

"Unless I'm mistaken," he said, "these documents tell whom they've been selling to."

Neil considered this as Harvey gloated over his next statement.

"Neil, Uncle Sam has been buying the entire crop."

Even in his confused condition, the disoriented newsperson realized Harvey was implicating the national government in a giant narcotics racket, a serious accusation.

"These papers have been signed by the president," Harvey continued. "It's all here—amounts, dates, prices."

Neil grabbed the folder and leafed through it himself.

"What the hell is Zenine?" he exclaimed, noting that all the transactions concerned themselves with this commodity.

"Zenine?" Harvey stifled a pained laugh. "Where have you been person?"

"Don't ask questions I can't answer," Neil replied. "Just tell me."

Too overwhelmed to argue, Harvey complied. "I've never tried it," he said, "but I've heard about it. It's a further refinement of heroin, just as heroin is a refinement of morphine. It's meant to be the ultimate high, but I don't know; it's very hard to get and very expensive."

Neil looked at the documents in his hand and shook his head.

"Well if these statements are to be believed," he said, "there should be an awful lot of it around somewhere."

Harvey's initial excitement was turning sour with in him, as if this information was radioactive and far too hot to handle. It was no mystery to anyone, even Neil, how violent and ruthless the drug barons were and this information would surely erupt in a national scandal of unprecedented proportions.

"Do you realize we're about to go to war over the Zenine trade and it appears we're the ones who have been financing the whole operation?" Harvey said angrily.

"What about Daisy Jr.?" Neil wanted to know. "Do you think he knows about all this?"

Harvey pondered for a minute.

"As far as I know, he retired after they resuscitated the president. Malt Sr. climbed into the saddle, took the reins, and Malter Jr. took a long overdue holiday. We were going to interview him from a historical perspective."

"So what perspective do we choose now?" Neil wondered.

"I don't know," Harvey said. "Who knows how long this has been going on?"

Neil was suddenly gripped by a deep despondency, the sort of despondency one feels upon discovering oneself to be the butt of a bad joke. If he were to chronicle his misfortunes, the last thing he needed was to be lost in a futuristic world, poised on the brink of war, and in possession of stolen state secrets that could incriminate the very man he was about to interview. As if this were not enough to contend with, he was about to have an experience few "outsiders" were privy to. With so much happening so quickly, he had not fully appreciated the implications of catching a space-zoot, but he was about to find out.

4

Kay Coincidentally Being
Her Name

Two hundred stories high, and with an area to match, the zoot terminal was a monstrous feat of engineering on a scale that rivaled the pyramids of ancient Egypt. Majestic, vacuous, it embraced the space like some medieval cathedral built in veneration of a mysterious god, and it more than lived up to its title of spaceport, encompassing, as it did, so much of it.

The Magnobile hissed to a halt, stopped by a blue-and-yellow clad official casually brandishing an exotic rifle and demanding, "Authorization!" through the tinted windows. Harvey produced two green plastic rectangles and was directed to take the *vater* to level nineteen, where the valet took charge of the car.

"Authorization?" the toothy blonde piped from behind the counter at the security gates. "Do you have anything to declare? Nuclear pocket calculators, aerosol spray cans, knives, guns, bombs, or high intensity particle beam weapons?"

Neil frisked himself quickly.

"Ah, no," he stated.

Harvey smiled self-confidently and shook his head. He waved the plastic rectangles and dragged Neil through the metal frame that constituted the security gate and headed to the departure lounge. They didn't get very far. Bells, sirens, flashing lights, and two large and sadistic security guards stopped them in their tracks.

The tooth lady climbed out from behind the counter and sauntered menacingly over to the two journalists.

"Not so fast boys," she hissed, speaking with an accent that sounded to Neil as if she'd been raised in the fifty-fourth state, which was Mars, according to the advertising hologram hovering above the security frame. The moon was the fifty-third. It had been incorporated into the Union in the year 2023, a privilege only half the Red Planet could boast; the other half having been claimed by the Russians for the reinstated USSR. Ownership of the celestial body had been a bone of contention for the entire century. The United States got there first, but the Russians claimed it was their color and felt the Americans would be better off on Venus. Needless to say, the Chinese claimed the entire planet for the People's Republic.

"Lets see those passes again, buster." She stood so close, Harvey could smell her breath: Juicyfruit. She chewed a few grinds and tucked the ball of gum into her cheek. Harvey fumbled in his pocket and produced the plastic cards.

"You boys better get used to the way we do things on the inside," she sneered and meandered back to her desk with a role of her more than shapely hips. Satisfied with the computer's verdict, she returned and delivered her report.

"You've got two minutes," she said, handing back the cards, and Neil wondered how he could have mistaken those fangs for teeth. Slipping the passes into his pocket, Harvey grabbed his partner and rushed down the hall, through the departure lounge and up the gangway. A guard, who removed his iPod earpiece as they approached, sat tilting back in his chair by the door to Cabin E.

"I know, I know," Harvey shouted petulantly, producing his plastic rectangles. "Authorization!"

The guard shook his head and replaced the earpiece with a smile.

"Ain't nothin' to me, person," he said passively. "I just work here."

Neil and Harvey weren't going to argue. With red lights flashing, they leapt through the hatch and fell sprawling into the cabin as two sets of doors popped shut behind them. Harvey picked himself up first. For him, this was just small change. Neil took a bit longer and was aided by a steward whose only comment was "Whoops-a-daisy," and whose broad, manicured moustache twitched as he straightened Neil's coat.

"Your seats are portside—"B" forty-four and forty-five," the wall computer dictated as the rectangles were fed into it. "Have a nice day."

"On the end," the steward indicated when they reached the appropriate row. Neil couldn't help but notice the next row of seats were vacant and stretched all the way to the wall. At the end of that row, a diamond-shaped window begged to be peered from. Harvey saw it too.

"Ah," Harvey mused. "Okay to move up a few seats?"

The steward's moustache twitched again, and with strained composure, he insisted, "The computer put you in these seats, and this is where you will sit."

"But they're empty," Neil protested with a wave of his hand.

"Yeah," Harvey said. "Maybe the computer's got Alzheimer's."

The steward was visibly agitated.

"The computer is not prone," he simmered, "to Alzheimer's."

"Look," Neil said, "we're not taking on any more passengers; what harm will it do?"

It was too much for the steward.

"No," he drawled out, almost melodically. "The computer has spoken." His face flushed hot pink. "Now sit down."

Neil and Harvey exchanged winks.

"Okay." They complied with resignation and squeezed their way along the row, clumsily treading on others' toes and apologizing profusely. As they sat, the lights dimmed and a holographic projection appeared above the front row of seats. It was the familiar image of Malt Daisy, leaning casually against his office desk and speaking to the camera.

"Welcome aboard the Trans-Daisy space-bus," he said. "The space-bus has been forging a tie with the universe since it was first developed earlier in this century. A giant electromagnetic catapult, it can land a reentry craft at Spacelands in just eight hours. You'll be making the trip our forefathers could only dream of. So sit back and relax. Remember, you don't have to worry about a thing. If anything goes wrong, we'll all be disintegrated in seconds. Enjoy your trip."

He was gone with a smile, and Harvey, noting all eyes, including Neil's, were riveted on the Donald Goose cartoon that had just commenced, elbowed his partner in the side and motioned to climb over their seats and sit by the window.

"Remember your own first law of journalism buddy," Harvey whispered as they settled themselves snugly in their new seats. "Never ask, the answer will always be no. Just do."

That's right, Neil thought. *That is my first law of journalism.* He leaned back in the well-cushioned seat and pondered for a while on this unexpectedly familiar thought.

Almost subconsciously he turned to Harvey and inquired, "What exactly is a space zoot?"

"It's the sound we make as we blast off." Harvey grinned, leaning over his partner and peering excitedly out the window.

"Blast off!" Neil didn't like the sound of that. "Wait a minute," he said, grappling with the implications. "Where the hell is Spacelands?"

"Well where do you think?" Harvey said, finding his partner increasingly tiresome.

The cartoon had ended, and the passengers were instructed to fasten their safety belts as the countdown commenced.

"Nine!"

Neil tugged on Harvey's sleeve as he struggled to tighten his belt.

"What, outer space?" he squeaked.

"We ain't goin' to Phoenix," Harvey said, fastening the catch on his belt and easing himself back in the seat.

"Eight!" the countdown continued. Neil went suddenly white, as if all his red blood cells had just packed up and gone on holiday.

"Seven! Six!"

"Wait!" he said, looking earnestly at his partner. "I forgot to turn the gas off; I'll be right back." He tried to leave his seat, but the belt held him down.

"Five! Four! Three!"

Harvey shook his head and laughed.

"Two! One! Shoot!"

The cabin lurched violently forward as the space-bus shot down the barrel of the catapult, pressing the reporters into their seats. As if every molecule in their bodies was being dragged backward, their flesh seemed to melt into the foam rubber cushions, meat and fiber squeezed together in a brutal embrace of unnatural intimacy. As the space-bus hurled itself into the daylight and soared upward, their bodies gradually began to assume their third dimension. Gravity eased its grip, and when he felt his eyeballs pop back into their sockets, Neil rolled his head sideways and threw his gaze out the window. He felt he'd very much like to throw his stomach out with it. The North American coast fell away beneath them like a disappearing map, the colors of its landmass fusing like impressionist brush strokes on a broad canvas. Where it met the dark edge of the ever-expanding horizon, the expanse appeared to glow a dull, toxic green.

Neil would have been sick there and then, but his stomach hadn't yet recomposed itself. However, as soon as it arrived some minutes later, he heaved into little brown plastic bags that hung like cavalry to the rescue from the back of the row in front.

"I'm gonna be sick," he complained lamely.

"You just were," Harvey observed.

"I'm gonna be sick again," he said. He was. He couldn't help himself.

It was just as well that they'd moved to the window away from the other passengers. Once the little girl regurgitated her milk and space-cookies all over her mother and the total stranger next to her, it was on for young and old. The man next to the stranger dove for his plastic bag, but it wouldn't tear free. He jumped up in panic and gushed forth the two eggs on toast, with onions, he'd devoured for breakfast on the bald head of the woman in the preceding row. She promptly stood up and punched him on the jaw, sending him flying into the lap of the young woman on the aisle seat, who irresistibly spewed her three breakfast sausages with gravy and French Fries, three monstrous servings of Special K (Kay coincidentally being her name), four cups of coffee, half a Sara Lee cheesecake, and a bar of Fruit and Nut Cocoa Milk Candy all over his gaping face. From there it spread like an outbreak of HIV in a Swedish sauna. People in rows throughout the cabin groped for brown plastic bags, and for those not fast enough, half the row would grope in empathy. Zoot shooting was hard yakka, even for the most experienced space traveller.

Lift-off was a draining experience, and the cabin settled down after the last carefully prepared breakfast had emptied itself into the collective consciousness. The two tenderfeet cosmonauts, feeling they'd left more than just their hearts in San Francisco, were drifting into a lazy, recuperative slumber when the patrolling steward spied them.

"Uh-oh, they've seen us," Harvey whispered. Neil moaned, his eyes were closed, his face a pale green.

"I think there's been some mistake." It was the head steward, Mr. Tarbo, with a clipped black moustache and greased-back hair, whose rotund body, like an upended football, bounced as he spoke.

"We must have been thrown out of our seats on lift-off." Harvey smiled nervously.

"I'm sorry," Mr. Tarbo replied, his outstretched hand demanding their tickets. "We have a special cabin for outsiders—strict company policy. Please follow me."

Too weak to argue, Harvey dragged Neil into the isle and propped his green, saggy body to attention. They swayed and stumbled like two drunks at closing time as they followed the head steward and came to a halt by the hatch where the computer had been.

"Do you see these?" Mr. Tarbo addressed the wall while indicating to the two journalists. "These men are outsiders and belong in Cabin Z!" He screamed suddenly and violently at the top of his suitably operatic voice, "You stupid, inanimate object!"

Regaining his head steward's composed dignity, he tugged at his lapels and motioned for Neil and Harvey to follow, leading them through the bank of commodes at the rear of the cabin—an area of much activity—and into the designated cabin where he sat them meticulously in their correct seats. Far beyond protesting, the two reporters were soon in a deep sleep. Having forgotten to fasten their safety belts, they floated around the cabin when zero gravity was reached and had to be strapped to their seats by the stewards. They were oblivious to the huge web of modules and scaffolding that floated to meet them from the black void above the Earth. And they were unaware of the space-bus backing into the docking bay of module seventeen. Not until the stewards were free to function in the artificial gravity of the module and able to rouse the groggy outsiders did Neil and Harvey regain consciousness. They were hustled from the bus like dazed sheep and directed, with a number of their fellow passengers, to the shuttle terminal for the outer satellites. They were left standing in long lines of passengers, grilled at clearance counters, submitted to the most invasive of medical examinations, and ferried to launch pads in a far sector of the module.

From the transparent, double-layered wall of the shuttle's departure lounge, Neil could see the front end of the pug-nosed craft hovering like a docked ferry with a glowing, starlit night sky as its backdrop. He leaned his face, wide-eyed and unshaven, against the clear plexiglass of the wall.

He wanted to leap out into the cosmos. What depth and glory! He could taste its beauty and feel his heart fly through the module and out into the infinity of space.

"It's beautiful." Harvey said, as he stood beside his friend and gazed at the panorama of the universe twinkling before their eyes.

"It's the most beautiful thing I've ever seen," Neil agreed, and they stood spellbound, drinking in the vision until they were shepherded aboard the shuttle.

As Harvey explained it, Malt Daisy III, known affectionately as Junior, kept his orbiting apartments on Plato, one of a half dozen or so man-made satellites that circled the Earth. Huge, revolving spheres—each was a metropolis—the ultimate extension of the suburban sprawl into the virgin vacancy of space. Controlled, contained, synthetic environments, they coexisted as minor planets unto themselves. Plato was one of the more sizable of the archipelago, and it housed the living and recreational areas of the ruling elite, a kind of Beverly Hills in a new world.

It was a five-hour journey by shuttle, two for those privileged enough to afford one of the latest model space hoppers, and a lifetime for two space-lagged outsiders with a big day ahead of them. According to Mr. Impiombartu, there was to be somebody there to meet them amongst the throngs of Platonians waiting to greet new arrivals. Eventually, as the crowd thinned and united parties departed, a short plump woman with a face like a hippopotamus and a disarmingly engaging smile, bustled up to greet them.

She was, she informed them, Malter Daisy's personal secretary, Gladdis Addis, though everyone called her Glad, and she was. She had come to show them to their apartments, where they would await Mr. Daisy's convenience and generally recover from the flight. She was bright and chirpy. In fact, she didn't stop talking from the moment she introduced herself to the time she closed the door on the two word-weary travellers.

If Glad was to be believed, Junior was the busiest retired old man on the planet. Much of her chatter concerned her own difficulty in keeping up with him as he shuttled between his Daisyworld home on the Red Planet and the satellites. He hadn't set foot on Earth in seven years, and she totally shared his humorous "why would I go back to that sewer?" mentality, as did a large portion of his fellow insiders.

"Air's better up here," Junior always insisted, and it was. Harvey and Neil could taste it. Thin, fresh, it was like the air at Healthlands and quite unlike the grimy humid soup that saturated his California apartment.

Succumbing to his journalistic curiosity, Harvey found a generously catalogued auto kitchen and promptly ordered two *Tribune* breakfast specials—two glasses of Scotch with ice. Without ice, they would have been *Tribune* dinner specials. They lounged around the spacious apartment, marveling to each other about the fantastic voyage they had experienced. It seemed all the more wonderful now that their stomachs had settled. Swelled with the euphoria of conquering the universe, they were soon joking as well about not wanting to return to that sewer, Earth.

After sampling a few more breakfast specials and then a few dinner specials, Neil drifted off to sleep while Harvey kept raving and stalking the apartment. Finally, he fell down the stairs that splayed into the adjoining gymnasium, from which he emerged several bruises the richer, and passed out on the couch. In the course of his slumber, he managed to fall off even this most spontaneous of beds and found himself, when he awoke quite some hours later, in a crumpled, vaguely Cubist heap on the floor. Neil was polishing off the last of his breakfast sausages and washing them down with an enormous mug of coffee from his adopted armchair.

"Glad was just here," he said between mouthfuls. "She said she'd be back in twenty minutes."

Harvey hauled himself onto the couch and sat up, massaging his scalp briskly with his long bony fingers.

"What time is it?" he yawned.

"I asked Glad that," Neil replied. "Do you want to know Earth time, Mars time, or lunar time? I think we're on lunar time."

"I reckon." Harvey laughed. He stretched his long gangly body and made for the auto kitchen. "Hey, with the moonshine this baby's putting out, no wonder nobody wants to go back to Earth."

"Take it easy on that stuff," Neil said. "We've got to go to work. He's ready for us."

"Fruito!" Harvey enthused and ordered a coffee instead. "Do you know what you're going to say to him?"

"What I'm going to say?" Neil hadn't thought that far.

"Well, don't look at me; I just take the pictures," Harvey said defensively.

Neil sat back. In the excitement of lift-off and the subsequent journey to Plato, he had lost sight of the fact that he still didn't know exactly who he was or what precisely they were meant to be doing. Embarrassed by his obliviousness to the enterprise they were undertaking, he squeezed his imagination to formulate a strategy.

"Say?" he formulated spontaneously. "Why, I'll ask him if he likes chicken soup and, ah, if he gets on well with his granddad."

"Uh-huh," Harvey grunted. "What about those invoices?"

"Invoices," Neil repeated. "Oh, yes." He drew the pages from his coat pocket. Harvey was about to suggest the use of a certain amount of tact, but in the moments before the words came to his lips, the door slid open and Glad breezed in.

"Shit, I thought you said twenty minutes," he said under his breath.

"That was twenty minutes ago," Neil slipped in under Glad's barrage of greeting.

"Oh, God." She laughed. "You boys look awful. If I looked that bad, I'd shoot myself."

Her belly wobbled and her shoulders bounced with well-humored hysteria.

"Why if I looked that bad in the mornings, I'd never get up."

Neil and Harvey looked each other up and down. They were disheveled, to be sure. They were unshaven; their hair was tussled and their clothes looked like they'd been slept in (because they had been).

"Well too late now. Mr. Daisy's a busy man," she declared, and marched the bantam press team, who were hastily straightening their ties and coats, out the door.

They tried to exchange a few last minute guidelines for the interview, but collaboration was rendered impossible by Glad's running narrative on the sights and features of her beloved home in the heavens. They stopped their pilgrimage outside an unassuming doorway in a miscellaneous corridor as Glad concluded, "If you'll wait in the foyer, I'll see if Mr. Daisy is ready for you."

Stepping gingerly over the threshold, Harvey withdrew the hand-held, fully automatic, industrial camera he unsheathed from his coat pocket, and rolled through a few minutes of film. The reception room had some notable features, such as Leonardo d' Vinci's portrait, *the*

Mona Lisa, and a large model of an exotic looking spacecraft floating in a domed ceiling. There were cultural artifacts and heirlooms, including a cigar store Indian and a glass display case boasting "General Custer's scalp", and another exhibiting the Shroud of Turin. He recorded it all as Neil posed in front of an abridged Japanese fountain bubbling from one corner.

"Okay, give us an intro," Harvey directed and raised the optic to his eye. Neil stared blankly into the lens.

"I'm not telepathic," Harvey stated. "Say something."

"Um, good evening," Neil said. "Well, here we are, a million miles out in space, in the private parts, ah, apartments, here on, ah."

"Plato, Plato," Harvey prompted in a loud whisper.

"Yes, Plato. Glad's gone to get Mr. Daisy, and then we'll, ah, talk to him." Harvey lowered the camera.

"Tell them about the invoices," he said, and resumed filming.

"Ah, the invoices." Neil pulled the pages from his pocket and waved them at the camera.

"Here I have some invoices that fell into my possession, ah, when I was in hospital. I had a bit of a mishap, with my head actually. I was talking to the president, and he had to have his heart cut out, so I stuffed these pages up my sleeve, it was an accident really, and it seems, ah, that he must have an enormous, ah, habit or something, because he buys millions of tons of dope—yes dope—every year. Here it is." He held a page towards the camera and indicated the signature with his finger.

"Right here, where it says, 'Malter Daisy, President,' and we're going to find out, ah, from a family member, um, if our president really is a junkie."

"Beautiful, beautiful." Harvey zoomed in for a final close up of Neil attempting to smile through his nervous perspiration. "The boss will love it."

"Harvey, I can't do this." Neil broke his pose and escaped to the center of the room.

"Can't do it!" Harvey pursued him. "Waddya mean? That was great. Now when we get in there, just take it slow and soften him up. Relax him. Get him to trust you. Then *whammo*! Lay it on him." Dangling the camera by its strap, he punctuated the *whammo* with a violent swing of his clenched fist into the palm of his hand as the double doors were flung open and Glad appeared. Her boss was ready to receive them.

5

Way Out of Their Depth
and Sinking Fast

AT THE FAR END OF a bare, olive green room, which was large enough to accommodate several offices, a solitary desk squatted beneath an imposing portrait of Malt Daisy. Behind it, in a high-backed leather chair, the throne of a corporate kingdom, sat the emperor himself, Malter Daisy III—Junior. Older than the old man Neil had met at Healthlands, but with a tight, sun-lamped complexion highlighting his colorless face, he looked more like Malt Daisy's grandfather than his grandson, though the resemblance was uncanny. He even had Malt Daisy's trademark thin moustache, and he styled his white hair with the same short cut.

After introducing themselves, the reporters sat in the two chairs awaiting them at the desk.

"So," Malter Daisy began. "You boys are going to interview me."

Neil looked to Harvey, Harvey looked at Neil, they both looked at Mr. Daisy.

"Yes," they chimed in unison.

"Who are you working for again?" Mr. Daisy asked, raising his eyebrows.

"*The Los Angeles Tribune*?" Neil directed the question at his partner, who nodded in the affirmative.

Not one to dilly-dally, Mr. Daisy prompted, "Well get on with it."

Neil turned to the camera, which Harvey hoisted to his eye, and began his introduction.

"Well, here we are again." He flashed a self-conscious smile across hot, flushing cheeks. "We have with us the man who took a simple amusement park and turned it into a national monopoly that today dominates every aspect of American life."

"Well I wouldn't put it quite like that." Malter balked defensively.

Failing to hear, Neil pressed on. "Yes, Mr. Malter Daisy III, and if I may say so, sir, you bear an uncanny resemblance to your grandfather."

Malter chuckled. "Well yes," he admitted. "You could call it something of a family tradition." He laughed again, and Neil began to relax into his newfound craft.

"Would you attribute this in any way to your grandmother's chicken soup?" he asked with apparent humor.

Malter slapped the table and guffawed in a manner reminiscent of his grandfather. "She made pretty good chicken soup," he said, and his hard, black eyes softened slightly.

Neil was beginning to enjoy himself and delivered the next question with the confidence of a seasoned veteran.

"And in your own words, Mr. Daisy, could you tell us how it feels to be the president's grandson?"

The softness disappeared from Malter's eyes and his brow furrowed pensively.

"Now look here, young man," he chided, evaporating Neil's steely veneer of confidence like ether on a hot day. "Don't you go forgetting who is responsible for putting the president where he is."

He glowered at the camera as if to acknowledge his awareness of it, and then he turned his attention to Neil, whose previously flushed features paled as he sunk into his chair.

"When I took control of the family business back in the early stages of the century, it was a mess—a bankrupt film studio and a waning amusement park. I took that studio and did what Malt Daisy had done a hundred years before. Only I did it bigger. The first, full-length, animated holographic cinema feature, and that was just the beginning. I built Daisylands in every city. Eventually, I built the cities. The single-structure, autonomous mega-city, we started that. Changed the face of America and the whole world followed. Young man, for fifty years I toiled to build up the company till it could no longer be said to exist within America. It was America." He paused, as if to underline the point and concluded. "Anyway, I'm not the president's grandson. He is Malter Daisy's grandfather."

Suitably rebuked, Neil groped to change the subject, and failed. "If you did all that," he said with softly barbed antagonism, "what did you need him for?"

"My boy," Malter replied, looking Neil square in the eyes. "Medicine has advanced a long way since granddad's day. Developments in cryogenics and the treatment of cancer enabled us to revive Malt and return him to a state of health he wouldn't have known since his youth. As a national icon, it was an easy victory for him to secure the White House and unify the presidencies of state and company into a family dynasty. It has enabled me to establish a new world on Mars and given me the freedom to devote all my energies to the colony there."

"On Mars!" Neil echoed skeptically.

"I wish I could take you there," Malter sighed, "but it's a three month trip. If you could only see the panorama of a Martian sunset, the kaleidoscopic fusion of all those poisonous gasses in the fading sun, you'd want to make it your home too, as I have done. And a very comfortable home it is too, don't you worry about that."

Neil shifted his weight awkwardly in his seat and Harvey rose from his chair, still filming, to crouch for the lower camera angle that lends an omnipotent feeling.

Malter continued, "Why we're as good as self-sufficient up there now. If the world blew up tomorrow, I doubt we'd miss you." He guffawed again.

"Do you realize that, even as we sit here, America is preparing to wage war with Latin America?" Neil volleyed, aware this was an imminent possibility.

"That's Malt's business," Malter answered briskly. "If he wants to go have a war, it ain't nothin' to us folks up here on Daisyworld. But in my opinion, the only good drug peddler is a dead'n. Molecular deunification of the entire continent would not be inappropriate."

Neil had no knowledge of Herman Fritzstein's discoveries in the field of molecular disassembly and reassembly, but his instincts told him he was better off in ignorance.

"Unless I'm mistaken, the club is meeting in just twenty-four hours to discuss that very issue." Malter thought for a moment then added. "But I'm sure Malt will do what's best for the country; he always does."

"Do you think it will come to that, sir?" Harvey spoke as he layed the camera on his chair and advanced toward the desk. "War?"

"Well what would you do?" Malter challenged him.

"To begin with, I'd stop ordering millions of tons of Zenine every year from them," Harvey fired back.

Malter was lost for a response. He wasn't sure he'd heard correctly.

"And just what do you mean by that remark?" he demanded when he found his voice.

Harvey shot a suspenseful glance at Neil, who returned it with sweaty recognition; the shit was about to hit the fan.

"Well . . ." He stalled. "What would you say if I told you I have proof the president has been acting as receiver for massive quantities of narcotics?"

Malter was visibly stunned but recovered himself and replied.

"That's an amazing allegation. You'll have to show me substantial proof before I could believe a preposterous story like that."

Harvey stood up to him defiantly.

"Show him, Neil," he commanded, reveling in the power he had at his disposal.

Neil was feeling more cautious and tried to communicate this to his partner by crossing his eyes, shaking his head, and contorting his face, all as discretely as possible. Harvey understood, but he was on a roll.

"No one's going to believe us if we don't show them," he whispered hotly. Neil was unconvinced. His instincts told him they were way out of their depth and sinking fast.

"I really think," Malter persisted, "if you have any way to substantiate a claim like that, you'd better do so, or I'll be forced to have both you and your journal charged with sedition."

It was a persuasive line of argument, and reduced by the beady determination of his gaze, Neil reached into his pocket and threw the incriminating pages on the desk. Malter sat down and scanned the evidence through dark-rimmed glasses he unfolded from his top pocket. Harvey resumed filming, and Neil waited apprehensively for a response. Eventually Malter removed his glasses and leaned into the corner of his armchair, stroking his moustache thoughtfully with one finger.

"How did you come by these?" he asked frostily.

"We're not at liberty to reveal our sources," Neil replied quickly, his own guilt dancing on the inflections in his voice.

Malter sat quietly for a while, intently eyeing the two journalists.

"The interview is over," he snapped finally, at which point a door slid open and a man, whom Neil and Harvey both recognized, strode into the room.

"My hopper's leaving," he said as he approached the desk.

"Ah, Jimmy!" Malter exclaimed, jumping to his feet. He appeared to be as nervous as the two reporters.

"Take a look at these." He passed the "evidence" to the secretary of state, who snatched the documents and leafed through each page.

"You found them," he said, beaming.

"These two found them," Malter corrected.

Having been totally oblivious to their presence, Jimmy stared at the two reporters, both white as sheets and shaking.

"And who are they? He asked.

"They're reporters." Malter gave in to his refined sense of black humor and laughed.

"What!" Jimmy screamed.

"They're from the *Tribune*," Malter added. "I think they're doing an exposé. They think Malt's been running drugs." He laughed again, but Jimmy was not amused.

Seeing them together, Neil suddenly realized the obvious.

"That's your signature, isn't it?" he accused Malter.

Malter smirked and preened himself briefly before replying.

"Malt may be president of the United States, but I'm still president of the company."

"Does anybody else know about this?" Jimmy interrupted, clasping his missing papers to his chest.

"Do you really think we'd be stupid enough to show you all this if we didn't have back up?" Neil stood up to Jimmy gamely, but the expression of horror on his face as he turned to face the camera testified that undoubtedly they were.

"You!" Jimmy shouted, looking Neil up and down. "You're that fruitcake from the hospital."

"I don't understand!" It was Harvey's turn to shout. "You're a drug runner?" His voice bristled with outraged indignation.

"Oh, come on," Malter whined. "You don't think you turn an amusement park into a national monopoly without a little business on the side, do you?"

"Why don't you tell them what we do with it?" Jimmy interjected sarcastically. "They only work for a nationally circulated news disc."

"They ain't goin' nowhere," was Malter's ominous response. Jimmy nodded grimly.

"What do you do with it?" Neil squeaked, his thoughts becoming words before he could stop them.

Malter placed his hands on the desk and leaned towards the quaking reporter.

"We put it in your water," he said triumphantly. Jimmy rolled his eyes to the ceiling. He didn't believe in being loose-lipped to reporters, no matter how dead they were going to be in twenty-four hours.

"We put it in your water, your food, everything we can supervise. We've been doing it for years." Malter was boasting. "Everyone on the outside, on the surface of the planet, you've all been junkies for years and you don't even know it yet. Well, the party's over. The cost effectiveness of the operation has exceeded the value of the gain. We're closing down shop."

"Gains!" Harvey screamed. "What possible gains can there be in juicing an entire country?"

"Think about it," Malter fired back. "Today, with a population of more than six hundred million desperate people, there'd be carnage if we didn't provide the citizens with the necessary medication to ensure a smooth and compliant social situation.

"It's not like it used to be. It's tough out there, you should know. The air stinks; the food stinks. It's grown in the ground, and that stinks. The place is a sewer. If you knew what was in every glass of water you drink, you'd kill yourself now and get it over with fast. In fact a war is just what the country needs to take its mind off the Zenine withdrawals. It'll be quite therapeutic really."

"Withdrawals!" Harvey bleated fearfully, devastated to discover he was a narcotics addict. "Does Zenine addiction have withdrawals?"

"You've heard of the expression 'cold turkey,'" Malter told him. "Try cold Botswanian ostrich."

Harvey's eyes widened, and he clutched his stomach.

"I think I feel it already," he said, beads of sweat breaking out on his forehead. "Get me some water!"

Malter laughed.

"You don't think we put that shit in the water up here do you?" He grunted disdainfully.

"You're sick." Neil shook his head in disgust.

"Sick!" the company president roared. "You're the one who's sick boy. I'm in perfect health. One hundred and four years old and never felt better, and I'll live another hundred before this body and mind are beyond the skills of our doctors. You'll be lucky to see your fiftieth birthday, you and all your pals on the outside. It wouldn't hurt if they made a nuclear crater of the whole country. How can you pollute a sewer?"

The two reporters fell back in their chairs. It was common knowledge on the outside that the soils and what remained of the reserves of water beneath the continent were hopelessly and severely contaminated with a wide array of chemical and nuclear toxins, as was the air. Everyone could see quite clearly that life expectancy for the bulk of the population had been reduced to fifty years or thereabouts, and it was generally known that the privileged technocrats who inhabited the country's seven enclosed, environmentally synthetic mega-cities and space-based satellites enjoyed a considerably higher quality of life. This disparity was played down by the Trans-Daisy Conglomerate and its appendages, such as the National Government.

"Glad!" Malter barked into his intercom. "Send for the house patrol."

It was a particularly threatening request, and Neil knew if they were going to do something, they'd better do it quickly.

"I wouldn't do that Mr. President." The title seemed to fit and came to his lips quite automatically. "I think you should know before you do anything rash; copies of these documents have been circulated to every media group in the country. If you don't call off the attack on South America, and return us safely home, they're going to publish."

He straightened up victoriously, and turning his back momentarily on Malter and the secretary of state, who were exchanging concerned glances, he winked at his partner. Harvey almost smiled in recognition of a possible avenue of escape.

"Now let's not be hasty," Malter said, doing some quick thinking himself. "Maybe there is room to negotiate. Sit down gentlemen, and let's see what we can work out."

He leaned toward the intercom and, flicking a switch, commanded, "Glad, cancel the house patrol and make up a pot of coffee. There's a good girl."

Neil and Harvey exchanged a mutual sigh of relief. Coffee sounded much less threatening than the house patrol, but then, they'd never sampled Glad's coffee. Huddling together and conferring briefly, Jimmy winked before disappearing through the side door. Malter reseated himself and smiled his best, wheezing-crocodile smile.

"Now let's take a look at this, shall we?" he said in a more conciliatory tone. "It's true we've been buying the entire southern continent's crop. With that revenue, they've managed to service their national debt; in fact, we now owe them. Big time. Why, without the proceeds of the international narcotics trade, they'd be even hungrier than they are now. And I can tell you they're already pretty hungry."

"That's because all their farming land is growing dope," Harvey explained to Neil, who shook his head sadly.

"Can't you buy the stuff off them and then destroy it?" asked Neil, naïve to the point of stupidity by any century's standards.

Malter grunted sardonically.

"Do you have any idea how much it costs to keep a population the size of the United States sedated for just one year?" he said.

It was all far too much for the uninitiated outsiders. Both felt as if the world had been pulled from beneath them, which, considering their position on the orbiting satellite, in a manner it had been. They sat quietly for some time, reflecting on all Malter had said and sipping occasionally from the cups of coffee Glad deposited on the desk.

"But what will become of everybody?" Neil implored when Glad had departed, thereby satisfying some illusion of confidentiality.

"It'll be a rude awakening when we stop supply, to be sure," Malter said, shaking his head. "I'm glad I won't be there to see it."

"But you've got to do something," Harvey pleaded.

"We've just decided to get out of the business," Malter answered.

"Well get back into it," Harvey shouted hysterically, still clutching his stomach.

Malter leaned back in his chair. "You realize," he said eventually, between gulps of coffee, "that if the American people discover what's been going on, they could rise against the government. It could mean revolution, war within and outside our borders. Is that what you want?"

The despondent reporters made no reply.

"There's no future back there boys," he continued. "The future's all up here. Maybe we could find you a job in the meat orchids or the loading bay for the space-freighters. The best thing you could do for your country would be to go back and tell them we've got everything under control. We're going to need a strong national spirit to get through the dark days ahead. Tell them that we're in this together and then come back and take your place with us in the new world. This is your ticket inside."

His face enticed them with its beaming wide black eyes and waited keenly for their response, but neither man said anything. Without warning, Harvey, who had decided anyone serving up coffee that bad could not be trusted, made a flying leap across the desk and knocked Malter and his high-backed chair sprawling beneath his own portrait. Neil jumped up as they struggled over the capsized hulk of the chair and ran to the other side of the desk. Tearing down one of the long banners that hung on either side of the painting, he wrapped it tightly around the company president.

Harvey grinned at his partner. "Quick, the side door," he said, and tucking the squirming, wrapped bundle under his own desk, they made their exit.

6

Why Can't You Use a Test Tube Like Everybody Else?

LIKE MICE IN A MAZE, the journalists scrambled through a labyrinth of corridors, eventually spilling into one of the periodic space parks that sprouted in hydroponic heaven from the synthetic environment of the satellite. Taking cover in a thicket of amply foliated greenery, they squatted and caught their breath.

"So what are we gonna do now?" Neil panted, wrestling an obstinate twig from his nostril. Harvey shuffled his long folded limbs and settled as comfortably as he could into the sanctuary of the thicket.

"We've got to get out of here," he said, also panting.

"Have you forgotten where we are?" Neil hissed back.

"Shush," Harvey said. "I know where we are. We're in a bush."

He shuffled again, but there seemed no way of avoiding the bush's thorny displeasure at their intrusion.

"We're a million miles out in space," Neil corrected, using a wider frame of reference, "in the middle of Ali Baba's cave. Believe me, the bush is not a problem."

As if to mock him, he was promptly flicked in the eye with a twig released by Harvey's shuffling.

"We've got to get back to Earth," Harvey whispered. "We've got to let people know what's going on."

"We were on our way until you clobbered Mr. Daisy," Neil said vehemently, blaming his partner for their predicament.

"Believe me, we're better off on our own," Harvey said with conviction. Neil shook his head.

"Who's going to believe us now that we've lost the documents?" he lamented.

"Don't worry," Harvey said softly, attempting to pat his holstered camera through his folded knees. "It's all here on the hard drive."

"Did you film all of that?" Neil shouldn't have been surprised. After all, Harvey was his cameraperson.

"Well, the camera was rolling." Harvey replied. "But don't ask me where it was pointing."

The sound of running feet terminated their discourse and climaxed as a trio of patrol officers jogged past the well-camouflaged fugitives.

"They'll be looking for us everywhere," Neil said as the sound of their jogging faded.

"Yeah, but they're not going to find us." Harvey was a born optimist. "One of us has to get this camera back to the *Tribune*. If only we had a hopper."

The space hopper had done for space travel what the Ford Model T had done for motoring. That neither man had any idea how to drive such a craft seemed a remote and trivial detail, and they quickly decided this was their best hope. Stepping from their prickly haven, they were brushing the clinging remnants of the bush from their clothes when the sound of voices froze them where they stood. From a clump of foliage not thirty yards away, two people strolled into view. They were walking at a leisurely pace, giving no indication they had noticed the two outsiders, who dared not move for fear of bringing attention to themselves. In the silence created by their stillness, the new duo's consternation could be heard quietly but distinctly. Although both were dressed in uniform body suits of grey and black, one voice was clearly a woman's.

"I mean really, Bernard," she was saying. "It doesn't even empty the ashtrays. Who wrote its program? Didn't you say one of your companies made it? Well of course they did. I mean who'd buy a domestic without knowing its background. That's not the point. It just doesn't do the job. I only ever get one sock back from the laundry. It wouldn't be so bad if the one that came back belonged to me in the first place, but even that's not what worries me. Bernard, it's the way it talks. I know the children like it because it sounds like Donald Goose, but I can't understand a word it's saying. The other day, after breakfast, it asked me if it should put out the trash, and I told it to put it down the garbage disposal because there were just a few scraps from breakfast. Bernard, it was talking about the cat!"

"Yikes," the male voice, which came from the smaller of the two, murmured. "There goes another endangered species." He saw the reporters first, standing just like another item of flora, and since they were now only yards from the path, he interrupted her monologue and bade them "good times."

The woman, who was as large and robust as her capacity for the spoken word, stopped talking and took account of the strangers.

"Good times," she greeted, as she and her partner reached that point at which the path was closest to them.

"Ah, yeah," Harvey responded hesitantly. Neil stood like a seized engine, unable even to blink. The small man smiled.

"Is everything all right?" he asked. He couldn't help but notice the aura of tension surrounding the two men. They looked guilty, and with the arrogance of the privileged, he presumed this was because of their obvious status as outsiders.

Outsiders were easily identifiable on the satellites because of their noticeably weather-beaten features, which contrasted starkly with the smooth and pale complexions of the well-manicured insiders. It was not common to see foreigners on Plato, and the man's question was motivated by curiosity rather than concern.

Harvey was about to assure the couple that everything was just fine when Neil gave vent to an insuppressible wail of hopelessness. The small man and his large spouse were visibly startled and stared at Neil, as did his partner.

"Good grief!" mumbled the small man, who was given to expounding expletives.

"It's okay; it's okay," Harvey shouted, prepared to deliver a rational explanation for why two outsiders were standing around screaming in far corners of a space park.

"Everything is fine. No sweat! Good times!" He stalled.

The woman made a few cautious steps off the path toward the two outsiders. Her face, which looked like it had been chiseled from the side of a cliff, screwed up in sympathetic anguish.

"Oh, dear, is your friend in pain?"

"No!" Harvey hastened to blunt her inquisitiveness. "Yes! He's sick; he's not well. He's . . . he's pregnant."

The couple looked truly astounded.

"He's pregnant! In fact, he's going into labor." He glared at his partner to play along, and Neil, who needed no encouragement, wailed again.

"He doesn't look pregnant," the small man scoffed through narrow lips.

"No, no." Harvey was stuck with it now. "The father was an African Pygmy, very small people. It's in there, and it's kicking to come out. What can we do?"

Neil wailed again, and Harvey persisted. "The only place that delivers male pregnancies is on the space base."

"Male babies?" the woman was thoroughly disgusted. "Well I know it's possible, but why can't you use a test tube like everybody else?"

For this, Harvey had no reply, so by surreptitiously kicking one of Neil's feet from under him and pushing him to the ground with a disguised helping hand on the shoulder, he knelt over his prostrate body and yelled over his all-too-genuine moans.

"We've got to find a hopper and get him to a doctor. How do we get to the spaceport?"

"Oh, the poor man." The woman turned to her husband. "Bernard! Drive them there in our hopper."

"What!" Bernard didn't share his partner's sense of charity or her extremes of gullibility.

"Bernard!" She reprimanded, her maternal instincts aroused. Bernard showed signs of resistance, so Harvey pressed home the deception.

"Oh thank you, thank you. We'll name the baby after you. Thank you! Please, help me get him up. Thank you."

The woman hurried over and gainfully assisted in hauling the mother-to-be to his feet. Her partner remained unmoved and held his position on the path.

"Name the baby!" he exclaimed. "What's it to you?"

Harvey looked bashful, then proud.

"I'm the father," he said, kicking the ground aimlessly with one foot. Neil screamed again, with increased ferocity, and the woman cradled him with one arm in a show of support.

"I thought you said the father was an African Pygmy." Bernard said, brazenly skeptical. "They're black, for starters."

"I'm an albino," Harvey fired back without hesitation. "I may be white outside, but I'm black inside."

Bernard's eyes narrowed, and though he didn't doubt the truth of this last statement, he couldn't help but observe Harvey was more than six feet tall. This time he thought he had him.

"Pygmies are little people," he said.

"Steroids," came the reporter's lightning reply. Neil began to howl for a doctor, and the woman grimaced in empathy. Her eyes appealed to her partner's compassion, but he was not a compassionate man.

"Goddamn!" she bellowed, and Neil could feel his eardrums wobble. "They're going to space base if I have to drive them there myself."

Clamping Neil firmly to her breast, she dragged him in the direction from which she and her husband had come, soothing him with pats and caresses and reassuring phrases such as "there, there" and "we'll have you there in no time."

Harvey followed close on her heels, walking briskly to keep up while Bernard's plaintive cries of "Ethel, Ethel" floated unheeded behind. Eventually giving chase, Bernard caught up with Ethel, panting with exhaustion as he ran to hold step with her. He would have needed a lasso to restrain her, so he had no choice but to follow.

Harvey lavished profuse amounts of gratitude on Bernard to thwart his lament about driving strangers around the solar system. Neil was being gratefully compliant, prepared as he was to suffer any indignity if it produced a passage back to Earth. He stumbled as he tripped between Ethel's forthright strides and cried out when his feet fell beneath her own. It all added to the theater.

They maintained a brisk pace and were making fine progress when a troop of the house patrol swung into the corridor ahead and jogged toward them. Neil closed his eyes and Harvey fell silent. The patrol leader noted the four hurrying people as they passed, but took no action and continued down the corridor. The two parties were thirty yards apart, and Neil had just opened his eyes when Bernard's voice rang out.

"Patrol, house patrol!"

The patrol stopped.

"Wait, Ethel, we've got help." Ethel stopped and about-faced, as did the house patrol, which jogged back and stood at attention before them.

"Soldier," Bernard commanded. "Take these men to the spaceport, berth QZ-23, and have my chauffeur pilot them to Space Base. Double-time. This man is pregnant."

The officer stomped and barked, "Yes, sir! Pregnant, sir?" he echoed, though it was not his to reason why.

"Double-time!" Bernard insisted loudly.

Bernard was none other than Bernard Krudd of Krudd Industries, a significant competitor of the Trans-Daisy Conglomerate until incorporation. Now he was a member of the board of directors. When he gave an order, it was obeyed.

Neil was wrestled from Mrs. Krudd after much resistance and marched, with Harvey, down the corridor. Bernard watched them disappear, delighting in ridding himself of them both.

"Albino pygmy," he cussed under his breath.

"I do hope it's a girl," Mrs. Krudd said wistfully.

7

About Those Spies, Sir!

THE HOUSE PATROL SLOWED ITS pace to a quick walk and continued through the honeycomb of corridors. Harvey cradled his partner as Mrs. Krudd had done and perpetuated her comforting. Neil moaned, pushing his stomach out as if swelled by the impending infant, and walked stiffly to give the impression of acute discomfort. It was a formidable piece of acting, the excellence of the performance, no doubt, owing much to the inspirational nature of the circumstance. He was, however, rehearsing in his head the precise manner in which he was going to tear his partner to pieces at the next available opportunity.

"Detail, halt!" the patrol leader screamed. The command was delivered in a tenor's range with a note that would have caused Neil to miscarry there and then had this charade been more than a ploy. The patrol leader about-faced.

"Wait here while I make the arrangements," he sneered, openly showing the utter contempt in which he held pregnant, male outsiders. Neil winced.

The Krudd's hopper was berthed on the promenade deck and had a socially respectable mooring. It was no coincidence, due to the Krudd's high ranking in the company's inner circle, that their hopper should share a berth with one of Malter Daisy's private fleet. It was something of a coincidence, however, that this very craft had been assigned to ferry the secretary of state back to Space Base.

Throughout human history, events have combined, time and again, in a fashion so intriguing and mysterious that many think divine

47

intervention accounts for such improbable twists of fate. But they fail to perceive that the random, untampered with, and totally accidental nature of coincidence is what makes the occurrence so wondrous.

The philosophies behind such happenings were not particularly important to Neil or Harvey as they stood surrounded by their company of patrolmen. But for whatever reason, or non-reason, it was a disturbing moment for both men when they realized the man who waited so impatiently with his own troop of patrolmen and several civilians some distance away was Jimmy, the secretary of state.

He shifted his weight awkwardly from one leg to the other, never remaining in one position for long, and glanced at his timepiece. The two spies had already delayed him and been the source of much anxiety. Having been notified of their escape, he didn't feel at all comfortable about leaving Plato while they were still at large, but the club was due to meet, and he could not be late. The troops of patrolmen who searched for the fugitives were numerous. Neil and Harvey had passed several on their way to the spaceport, but their overt presence did little to mollify the secretary of state. He looked around constantly in all directions, as if it were his personal duty to find and apprehend the enemy agents.

It was as much surprise as joy when he spied them, cringing behind their escort, and with his entourage close behind, he hurried over to where they stood and barked triumphantly at the guards.

"Ah, you've got them. Excellent, Thomas!" He turned to one of the civilians who separated like an amoeba from the entourage. "Have them call off the search and have word sent to Mr. Daisy that the spies have been arrested."

Thomas nodded his head with comprehension and took his leave with a quick bow that hinted at the adoption of some Asian custom. Jimmy turned back to the guards and, singling out the patrolman on the right, bellowed with the authority of a company sergeant.

"Where's your patrol leader?"

"Sir!" The patrolman stomped his right foot and saluted by placing his outstretched palm beside his right ear.

"Our senior has gone to prepare the Krudd hopper to take these men back to space base. Mr. Krudd's order's, sir!"

Jimmy seemed suitably impressed.

"Excellent, excellent," he said. Then, addressing the plainly clothed men behind him, he boasted, "Now that's what I call efficiency. Thirty minutes and our birds are back in the cage. Those outsiders don't stand a chance against that sort of organization."

"Sir!" The soldier who addressed the secretary of state appeared to be concerned about something. "This man is pregnant, sir!"

Jimmy looked hard at Neil, who was perspiring profusely and smiling hysterically through gnashing teeth. In a silence more pregnant than he would ever be, he waited for the delayed response of the secretary. Jimmy recoiled from his crazed eyes.

"Congratulations," he said finally.

Neil was slowly retreating to a sub-catatonic state and was incapable of responding with so much as a thank you.

Jimmy was indifferent—Harvey thought he might have detected some jealousy—and when a port official appeared and announced his hopper was ready, he instructed the escort to carry on and departed. Neil and Harvey had a long wait in which to ponder their position. Harvey considered making a break for it, but mindful of Neil's catatonia, which he could ascertain from the glaze of his eyes, and the daunting presence of the patrolmen, he thought better of it. When the patrol leader returned, the chauffeur's copilot, Maurice, accompanied him. Puffy-eyed with tousled hair and sagging jowls, he looked like he'd just woken up and was none too sober.

"Okay, you two, you're on your own. Maurice here's gonna drive you home," the patrol leader sneered.

Maurice gathered his concentration and slurred, "This way." Then he lead the quietly frenzied outsiders up the gangway. They had barely disappeared when the soldier who had been addressing the secretary of state stepped forward, stomped, and saluted.

"About those spies, sir!"

"Don't worry about them; they've been caught. We can go back to the barracks. Detail attention!"

"But, sir!" the soldier protested, but the patrol leader had no patience with subordinates.

"Dweyer!" he screamed. "Shut up! Troop, about-face! Forward march!"

And forward march they did without hearing the young patrolman's suspicions about the identity of the expectant couple. They trained their troops diligently on the inside, and it was quite automatic for him to accept the directives of his leader without further questioning. This didn't prevent him, however, from holding the unsettling conviction that he and his comrades had been unwitting dupes in a bizarre comedy of errors.

8

The Lusty Blue Eyes,
the Rosy Curve of Her Lip

MAURICE STUMBLED THROUGH THE GANGWAY and swayed as he turned to enter the cabin. Neil and Harvey had to help him into the pilot's seat, and they woke him twice before they blasted free from the berth and out into the infinite darkness. When they were satisfied their course was secure, and with assurances of returning at an agreed upon hour, they left him to catch forty winks and retreated to the passenger cabin.

Colored in deep crimson with wallpaper featuring patterned repetitions of the Krudd corporate logo, and bathed in a soft silvery light, the cabin was a luxurious respite. The two exhausted reporters collapsed into the plush divans hugging the mildly convex walls and stretched, taking large gulps of air and filling their lungs with the sweet taste of freedom. Harvey began to laugh—a ridiculous giggle of disbelief at first, growing to an unrestrained belly laugh that shook his whole body. Neil was silent but for his heavy breathing, and it was some time before he rose to a sitting position. Harvey sat up, too, and with a wry smile creeping across his face, he looked at his partner. Without warning, Neil leapt from his seat, and with a primeval scream, he seized Harvey around the neck, knocked him to the floor, and beat his head repeatedly against the cushion of air carpet.

"This is all your fault. You're crazy. I'm crazy. They're all crazy!" He laughed diabolically as Harvey struggled to wrest the squeezing hands from his throat.

"This isn't even real. Why, it's a goddamn nightmare." He continued pounding the floor with Harvey's head. As suddenly as he had attacked, Neil loosened his grip on his dazed accomplice and jumped to his feet. Harvey coughed and gasped for air as he eased himself against the side of the divan.

"That's it!" Neil was having an epiphany. "This is just a bad dream. Yeah. A nightmare. This isn't really happening at all. You're not really here."

He looked at Harvey rubbing his neck gingerly from the floor.

"We're not really in a space ship. Malt Daisy isn't really president of the United States. And we're not about to go to war over an international drug trade. Why, I'm not even pregnant."

He breathed a huge sigh of relief and stretched, filling himself with his own sense of masterfully restored sanity. Then he strode around the cabin, mocking the portrait of Malt Daisy above the beverages dispensary and defying the horizon of the Earth that arced in a shimmering glow of light behind the portholes on the starboard side. He returned to the center of the cabin and stood triumphantly before Harvey, who by this time had pulled himself up to his full height and towered over his partner. Calmly, the gangly reporter reached into his pocket and produced a box of matches, unceremoniously striking one and pressing the burning end into one of Neil's fists, which swaggered astride his hips. The sulphur crackled and burned into his flesh, filling the immediate area with the nauseating aroma of burnt meat. Harvey batted not so much as an eyelid as Neil hopped around the cabin, doubled up in agony and swearing at the top of his lungs.

"Sorry, I thought you were dreaming," he said innocently. Neil clutched his smoldering hand and fell into one of the divans, writhing like a dying beast. His howls descended to whimpers, and his reflex for revenge was tempered by his deeper confusion as to how he came to be flying through space on a mad quest between worlds in which he was a stranger. He was beyond caring what happened to his body, to the *Tribune,* or to the world. Each time he had slept, he had woken in the hope of finding himself in his own bed, in his own suburban bungalow, ready to drive to work in the beetle on a beautiful California summer day. With each awakening, and by finding himself well anchored in a time he found so hard to accept, he felt his visions and memories becoming more like distant dreams. They hung in his semiconsciousness like the veiled promise of a happier reality.

"I wanna get oughtta here," he moaned, "and I don't want to go back to friggin' Daisyville and have a war."

Harvey easily concurred with these sentiments.

"Can I tell you something, Harvey?"

Harvey was obtuse to the sensitive honesty released by Neil's deeper psychological anxieties.

"I don't understand any of this—this space travel. The single-structure mega-city, cars that drive themselves, you, Malt Daisy. A week ago, I was a happy young man, living at the turn of the century for Christ's sake. I was writing editorials for the *Tribune*, which was a newspaper. You know, words? I had a wife, a house, and a car. We went to the beach on the weekends."

Neil stopped. Harvey was being very patient, but even to himself he sounded ridiculous. He lay quietly after this outpouring, the last vestiges of resistance to accepting his situation slowly dissipating.

Harvey said nothing. He understood now why Helen had been so insistent Neil should not go with him. He realized it must have been a serious head injury to have so affected him.

"Now look, old buddy," he said, "I don't know what they did to you in that funny hospital, but the fact of the matter is, this is not a dream, and it's too important for us to walk away from. When we get to space base, I suggest we make a bolt for it and get lost in the crowd. They're bound to put two and two together and be waiting for us at the other end."

Neil's mind was wandering again. He half listened to and agreed with all Harvey's plans, nursing his hand tenderly and staring through the dark portholes as if hypnotized. He wanted to go back to Earth, but he didn't want to return to the world he had regained consciousness in. He felt he had no home, no place to go, no past, no future, and a present he couldn't recognize.

Time passed quickly, and at the appointed hour, Harvey roused Maurice, who was snoring obscenely over the controls. He was still groggy, but perceptibly clearer after his nap. He even wanted to know if Neil had gone into labor yet, and kept asking, all through the docking procedure, if the contractions had started. It appeared Maurice had gone through something similar when he and his girlfriend were marooned in a far-flung lunar resort some years earlier.

The docking went without incident and when their moorings were made fast, the intrepid reporters shook the copilot by the hand and disembarked through the center hatch. Harvey had been right about one thing. They had put two and two together right after Malt Daisy rang Bernard Krudd to thank him for capturing the outsider spies. It was news to Bernard, who immediately realized he'd been duped. Too embarrassed to reveal details of the subterfuge, he concocted a wild tail of assault and theft, and the alarm bells were rung, by which time Neil and Harvey had already reached the Earth-bound space-bus terminal and managed to disguise their presence by joining a group of outsiders on a package tour of the moon.

The moon served the valuable function of a tourist resort for insiders and outsiders. Fun-seeking vacationers kept the facilities booked all year round with deals ranging from weeks with the whole family to lightning-fast, round-trip, three-day Earth-to-Moon tours. It was in the midst of one such tour that the paranoid reporters camouflaged themselves and their identities as outsiders.

They gathered from the excited conversations by tour group members that the tour guide was organizing their places on the space-bus. They were a spirited band of adventurers, numbering between fifteen and twenty, and they unhesitatingly embraced the reporters as members of their troop. Neil and Harvey willingly accepted the assumption, and it was as they were deliberating on whether or not to use the tour as a screen to smuggle themselves back to Earth that Neil saw her standing on the far side of the terminal.

She was young and fresh; her short, blond hair framed her rounded features like a cherub from an Italian master's canvas. She was not tall, and her figure, though far from slender, was shapely. Her snappy blazer fit like a glove with two fingers and her dark-blue, almost knee-length skirt stretched tight as she straddled her colorful carry bag that lay on the ground between her legs. It was Helen.

Even from a distance he recognized her immediately. Not the Helen who picked him up at the hospital, but the Helen he remembered from those elusive days before the accident. She hadn't changed at all. It was the same hairstyle she had worn the morning he kissed her goodbye and set off to cover the anniversary celebrations at Daisylands. She hadn't aged a day; in fact, as she glanced around the terminal—as if she were waiting for someone—she looked younger than he remembered.

Neil was spellbound, and before he knew what he was doing, he found himself walking in her direction. Harvey, who was exchanging pleasantries with a middle-aged woman from the tour group, was unaware of his departure.

He drew near and was bewitched by her lusty blue eyes and the rosy curve of her lips. His heart began to pound in his chest, and he remembered the day they first met. Helen had been up to her thigh-high gumboots in pig shit down on the farm, smiling like a daisy on a sunny, sunny day. It was hard for him to know what to say, so much separated them in this strange place. He could scarcely believe he'd found her at all. She made no recognition of his hovering presence before her, only straining to see around him. Something was causing her distraction, and she kept glancing at the departure index, splayed out in holographics above them.

"Helen!" Neil blurted finally in an attempt to attract her attention. She cast him a passing glance and consulted her timepiece. "Helen Cradley from Fredsburg Wisconsin."

Helen looked up. Their eyes met, and Neil's heart jumped into his mouth. She was less impressed.

"I'm sorry; I think you've mistaken me for someone else." Her manner was polite and direct and not at all typical of her usual bouncy friendliness.

"You sure as hell look like her," Neil said.

"I wouldn't be too sure of anything related to hell," she said. "Please excuse me. I can't wait for him any longer. I've got a space-bus to catch."

She picked up her bag and, swinging it over her shoulder, headed off through the gates for the East Coast Zoot.

Neil watched her disappear through the doorway; all his visions and memories of a saner existence disappeared with her. He glanced over to the tour group, where Harvey had just noticed his absence. The tour leader, having returned, was hurrying the members off in double file, including Harvey who was so intent on relocating his partner, he was oblivious to his pairing off with the middle-aged lady he had been talking to. By the time Harvey spied Neil standing under the departure index, he was being marched off with the rest of the group.

Neil cupped his hands and shouted, "See you at the *Tribune*." Then he raced through the doors after Helen, down the corridor, and with the familiar red light flashing, he flung himself through the gangway seconds before the doors zipped shut behind him.

9

Space Base Station

MORE DAZED BY THE IMPLICATIONS of his separation from Harvey than by the fall, Neil sat on the floor of the space-bus until a pair of hands lifted him with a familiar "whoops-a-daisy." Mr. Tarbo strode up behind the back row of seats and addressed the steward, whose moustache twitched as he straightened Neil's jacket.

"What's happened here then?" he demanded to know. The steward took a step back and, seizing Neil by the shoulder, spun him around to face his superior.

"Oh, it's you again," Mr. Tarbo said with distaste. His trimmed black moustache was developing a twitch of its own, and for some moments, they stood there, both moustaches twitching ferociously, until Mr. Tarbo broke the silence.

"Do you have your ticket?"

Neil had no ticket.

"Gee, I must have dropped it in the fall."

"Then I'm afraid you'll have to fall out, too, until you find it." Mr. Tarbo ran a very tight ship.

"But we've already left," Neil protested.

"Not quite." Mr. Tarbo clicked his heels and slicked back the greasy shock of hair on his left side with the palm of his hand.

"Roberto." He gestured to the steward to throw Neil out with a flick of the finger and a spin of the wrist—an order Roberto was about to carry out when Neil cried, "Wait! That lady who just came in—she's got my ticket."

The steward looked to his superior for instructions. Mr. Tarbo cocked an eyebrow skeptically.

"That woman is Janet Kennedy. She's the secretary of the Department of Small Furry Animals," he said.

"Well she's got my ticket." It was only a hunch, but if she'd been waiting for someone who didn't turn up, Neil figured there was a fifty-fifty chance she had both tickets. Escorted personally to the VIP lounge by the officious head steward, Neil was presented to the secretary of small furry animals, who was obviously expecting someone else.

"But you're not my secretary. Where's Victor?" she said indignantly.

"Ah hah!" Mr. Tarbo snapped.

"That's what I was trying to tell you in the terminal." Neil was thinking fast. "Victor's caught the dreaded spacelurgy. Everybody's coming down with it. He sent me to fill in for him. Malters is the name." He reached down and shook her hand. "Er, Malter Malters, pleased to be working with you."

"Oh fine," she murmured and withdrew her hand. Mr. Tarbo, seemingly unsatisfied, looked disapprovingly at Neil then back to Janet.

"That will be all, steward," she instructed, and with a curt attempt at a bow, Mr. Tarbo retreated to the economy cabins.

"Well don't just stand there," she spoke to Neil. "Sit down. We'll be leaving in a few minutes."

Her manner was brisk and business-like, and Neil sat down quickly, fearing the rigors of another blast off. He was to be pleasantly disappointed. The return trip was a simple glide back to Earth without the imperative to blast free from the Earth's gravitational pull. Once on their way, he relaxed and glanced around the cabin, noting the VIP lounge was similar to the Krudd's hopper, an unsurprising fact to those who knew Krudd Aerodynamics had built the space-bus; but of course, Neil didn't.

Movement around the cabin, though strictly forbidden in the economy cabins, was accepted in the VIP lounge. Anyone who could afford the appropriately astronomical fare was a very important person and his or her whims were catered to. As a result the lounge was connected to the space ballet room by way of a circular hole in the wall. Gyrating to space-disco music during zero gravity, off all sides of the room, including the ceiling, had become something of a fad amongst the affluent young boppers of the twenty-first century.

Neil, who had not yet strapped himself in, floated to the ceiling as soon as they cleared the artificial gravity of space base. He was projected from his seat by his butt's belch of appreciation for the lunch Harvey had prepared for them from the galley of the Krudd's Hopper. Enjoying himself until Janet's matronly "oh, for heaven's sake" sent him floating back to her side, he seized the strap of his seat belt and tied himself firmly to the sofa.

"Are you having a good time?" she said sarcastically.

"Yes, I think so." Neil was being honest.

"Victor is indispensable to me. Do you think you can handle this?" Now she was being skeptical.

"Oh yes, I think so." Neil wasn't being honest anymore, but it seemed sufficient the first time, so he thought he'd say it again.

"This is a very important Cabinet meeting we're going to. I really don't see how Victor expects me to manage with an uninitiated secretary at this stage." She was becoming quite petulant.

"Victor had no choice," Neil explained.

"Just like a man—whenever you need him . . ."

Neil had no idea, but in fact Victor had not come down with the dreaded spacelurgy. He had simply overslept after a heavy session the night before at Space Base Station, the swingingest, booziest, pill-poppingest, sleaziest nightclub in the satellite archipelago.

Neil looked at her. He forgot everything else when he was in her company. None of it mattered. Harvey, the *Tribune*, even his own confusion over his own identity. He would drop it all and start anew if he could be with her.

"Never mind," she said, "get your computator out. I want to alter my speech to the Cabinet."

"Computator?" Neil queried.

"Yes. Didn't he give you his computator?"

"There wasn't time." Neil squirmed, having no idea what she was referring to.

"Really!" Her temper was quicker than he remembered and her patience, which she always had in abundance, seemed strangely absent.

"Well what am I supposed to do now? It took me days to write that speech, and you left it behind."

Neil could see they weren't getting off to a very good start and felt he'd better do something quickly to salvage the situation.

"That speech was wonderful." He lied. "Victor quoted extracts from it over the phone. Brilliant. It was so, so succinct. So effortlessly articulate. I'm sure you can remember it. What was that opening line?"

Flattery was always a good place to begin, and cajoled by these compliments, Janet collected her thoughts.

"Well," she began, "it went something to the effect of, 'Fellow members, Mr. President. I know you all feel strongly about this issue, and I am in total sympathy with your sentiments regarding these crimes against humanity. I agree the trade in narcotics must stop and those involved brought to justice, but to initiate a continental war can only mean one thing, the death of millions of furry animals and the destruction of their habitats throughout both South and North America. Heavens knows there are hardly any left out there as it is. Do you want your children to grow up and not know what a puppy dog is? May I remind you that Mickey Moose himself was a furry animal?'"

She ceased her monologue and looked at Neil. "That bit should really get them." She winked.

Neil felt dazed and more than a little amazed. By now he just accepted that something in his brain had short-circuited, but he really didn't know what to make of her speech, and when he thought about it, he couldn't recall any tradition of government portfolios for small furry animals. He wanted to be encouraging but wasn't at all sure how to go about it.

"Oh, what came next? Now I've lost my concentration." She thought for a moment. "I remember. I wanted to scrap all that stuff about organizing a rally of furry animals in Washington Park. I don't think we'll have time to do the necessary leafleting." Neil nodded. "Instead, I wanted to add a whole new angle. What do you think of this?"

Neil braced himself.

"'Mr. President, instead of making war on Latin America, why not treat governments like businessmen and come to some arrangement? Buy them out if necessary.'"

If only she knew what she was saying, Neil thought.

"Well what do you think?" she asked him, eyes excited.

"Think? I think it's a great idea," Neil responded. "Why, we could buy the entire crop and burn it."

"Well there's no reason to waste it. It has marvelous medical applications in the field of veterinary medicine," she countered.

Neil didn't know what to say.

"Think of all the cattle and sheep that could be humanely put to sleep at the abattoirs."

"You know, sheep aren't strictly furry animals; they're sort of woolly," Neil observed academically. Janet took no notice and went on.

"Animals could have general anesthesia during surgery. Catnip would be a thing of the past. We could have things like dognip, fishnip, hamsternip."

Neil caught the eye of a steward who was floating past and ordered a nip of bourbon with Coke.

"There's no end to the uses for it. Why with the marketing profits, we could help the furry animals in South America as well as in the United States. Did you know there are nearly a billion starving people down there? They even eat each other. Those poor animals don't stand a chance, and that's why this department is definitely against the proposed action."

"Do you get along with Malter Daisy Jr.?" Neil asked bleakly.

"I don't see him often but yes, we get on very well. Why?"

"Nothing," Neil dismissed, unnerved to find himself consorting with the enemy, but relieved she opposed the war. This at least was some common ground.

"I fear all of this will fall on deaf ears. They're set on going in there shooting." Janet returned to the subject. "I've never seen the secretary of state move so quickly and comprehensively on any other issue."

"Excuse me, but when you say they." Neil sought to disguise his ignorance as gracefully as possible, "you mean . . . ?"

"They," Helen snapped, "the members of the club."

"Of course." Neil nodded.

"They want blood."

"Yes, blood. You're not a member of a Satanist cult are you?"

Neil was trying to make light of the topic, and Janet was enraged.

"I'm a member of the government of this country and your boss. Remember that, Mr. Malters." She had the glare of a head mistress, and Neil wilted under her authoritative gaze.

Having had little time to rest as she prepared for the club meeting, Janet settled back to sleep for a few hours while Neil sipped his bourbon and Coke through a one way straw and watched as other passengers floated back and forth between the space-disco room and the cabin. He battled his impulse to join them, but he lost—so join them he did, on the dance floors. People were flying in all directions, flailing hysterically in slow motion to the pumping space-disco rhythm. The colored holograms were pulsing in splashes of light, the strobe flickered, and excited dancers screamed over the music. Neil screamed too.

As Earth's gravity began to impose itself, the exhausted and exhilarated dancers returned to their seats. Some braved the raised bar area at the back of the cabin, where they sipped on their spherical cups, which looked like huge, colored Ping-Pong balls, and tried to maintain their balance as the space-bus reentered Earth's atmosphere.

Swept up in the momentum, Neil found himself partying with a group of law students from Michigan who were letting their hair down and taking full advantage of their end-of-semester break. Like most law students, they enjoyed themselves in a wholesome and bawdy display designed to deny the general image of the boring, girlie, swat-law faculty, but it served only to advertise the fact. They laughed and told inane stories about the eccentric habits of their various professors and other farfetched tales, forming a framework in which Neil's ravings about being a time-traveler were just part of the conversation.

By the time they were preparing to land, Neil was so intoxicated, he thought they were still at zero gravity and launched himself into the air from the back of his seat, falling heavily to the floor to the thunderous applause and hilarious cacophony of his party of students. When he opened his eyes and looked up, he saw that he had landed right in front of Janet. With stubble forming the beginnings of a crusty beard, his head plastered with thinning locks of sweat-battered hair, and bloodshot eyes that stared with an apologetic air of inebriated good humor, he picked himself up off the floor and rolled into the sofa beside her.

"Good bourboning." He burped.

Janet took one look at her new secretary and knew it wasn't going to be an easy meeting.

10

Script!

THE CABINET WAS TO CONVENE in Washington, DC, at the Fantasy Castle, a representation of the famous castle at the Daisylands amusement park on a spectacularly large scale. Dwarfing the old city of Washington that sprawled to one side of the four walls which comprised its battlements and central structure, it cast a shadow as black as the glass from which it was fashioned.

It was a bizarre palace, glinting like a mirage in the afternoon sun, a monolithic tribute to a new America. The tops of the ramparts were used as landing strips for incoming aircraft, and it was on the top of one of the corner turrets that the commuter jet from the spaceport landed.

Janet was far from impressed with the conduct of her new secretary. His entire voyage on the commuter jet had been spent in discomforted convalescence over the toilet bowl as his drinking's excesses took their toll on his biorhythms. After they landed, she was ushered away quickly to a debriefing session with other club members—they called it rehearsal—and Neil was sent to sober up and wash.

Bewildered by his experience of space travel, he was subconsciously euphoric at being back on the terra-firma of Earth, a celestial body he was now aware he loved as much as life itself. It was the womb of conception of all life in the solar system. It was his home and housed the dust from which he was made and to which he would return.

Having showered and shaved, he watched news updates on the staff room holovision and learned that the club met every month, but it had been called early due to the state of emergency. It was always broadcast live in the democratic tradition of openness, or more subtly, the totalitarian tradition of propaganda, and was keenly watched by the entire insider population.

Neil knew what he had to do. Taking heart from her apparent naïveté, he resolved to challenge Janet with the truth about the drug trafficking, and by so doing, reinstate himself to a position of grace with her. But time was running out, and it was not until the very stroke of six o'clock that he burst into the Moose Hall, where the Cabinet meeting was poised to commence.

Through the activity of the camera crews who glided across the studio floor, Neil could see the Cabinet members arrayed behind a semicircle of desks, baking in the glare of the stage lights. In the center of this half circle, his chair raised at the back above the others, and unencumbered by a desk, Malt Daisy gazed at the studio audience who filled the amphitheater of the hall.

The ethereal silence was broken when Jimmy, who stood center stage and was surrounded by fellow members of the club, gestured to a technician. The hall shook as the sound system reverberated to the opening strains of "The Mickey Moose Club" theme song.

"Who's the leader of the gang . . . ?"

The music proceeded through the entire piece as showers of confetti and balloons rained from the ceiling. A costumed Mickey Moose and Donald Goose danced onto the set with a host of other Daisy characters and as the song built to its climax, streamer cannons laced the stage with colored bands of paper.

Without missing a beat, Jimmy yelled as the last bar finished, "Hello boys and girls, and welcome to the *Mickey Moose Club* 'Overt Action Special.' It's going to be a hot little show tonight, so let's get going. I'll be with you all the way. You know me, I'm Jimmy!" and in a militarily precise maneuver, the occupants of the desks moved in single file to the front of the stage. The first of them passed in front of the secretary of state.

"And I'm Bobby," he said. The others followed in turn, announcing their names and smiling from beneath the bar of moose antlers that straddled their Mooseketeer caps.

"Karen, Victor, Scott, Horronomus, Janet." It continued until all were accounted for and ended when Malt pontificated from his throne.

"And I'm Mickey." He placed his Mooseketeer cap on his head as if it were a crown and sat in a chair winged with a sprig of moose antlers.

Several cameras mounted the stage and glided in for close-ups of the president as the studio audience, instructed by cue cards, clapped and cheered. Released from the ceremony of the anthem, they seated themselves and the president began his opening address.

"Club members." His voice was heavy with the gravity of the occasion. "We are called together today because of an urgent and horrific matter. I refer, of course, to the international trafficking in narcotics." He paused as a ripple of indignation trickled its way through the audience.

"When a country that can't even feed itself devotes all its resources to the cultivation of these poisons it uses to destabilize its neighbors, it is an odious and despicable crime that can't go unpunished. We will hear the options that are available to us from each of our members and take a vote in the spirit of democracy, which made this country great, But first, here is the cartoon."

The cameras panned back as the stage was splashed with the color of a Daisy animated holographic feature. Now was his chance. Edging his way backstage, Neil found Janet in the wings, still trying to remember her speech. Upon seeing him, she gave expression to pent up anxieties and poured them over her inept secretary like a bucket of human excrement.

"Where have you been you bozo? Where's my speech? Where's Victor!?"

"Helen!" Neil shouted in a loud whisper. "I mean, Janet!"

Janet ceased her vitriol.

"It's okay, I remember the speech. I have a brain like a computator. That's why Victor sent me. Now repeat after me."

Janet looked impressed and, taking a deep breath, nodded for him to start.

"Mr. President." Janet repeated after him. "The Trans-Daisy Conglomerate has been bleeding the wealth of the nation to build themselves a luxury escape on Mars. They've been controlling the narcotics trade and left us with the bill."

"Wait a minute." Janet stopped him. "That's not my speech. Mr. Malters, in twenty minutes we're going to democratically vote yes to have the entire Southern Continent disassembled. This is not a joking matter."

"Vote yes?" Neil was as incensed as he was surprised. "What about all the furry animals?"

Janet shrugged.

"Better theirs than ours," she said. "Anyway, it's in the script."

Scripting democracy was an innovation Neil didn't want to consider.

"Ms. Kennedy," he said, going to the heart of the matter. "Malter Daisy Jr. and the secretary of state have been running this narcotics racket from the beginning. They confessed this to me themselves."

Janet took a step back and glared at him.

"You're crazy," she said, glancing around for help.

Neil could see she was panicking, and by reflex did what he had done the night he proposed. Walking up to her, he whispered, "I love you," in her ear and gave her a long and passionate kiss on the lips. Released from his embrace, Janet took another step back and slapped him hard across the face.

"I'm calling the police," she said.

Neil had just stepped over the line. By kissing a woman without her permission he had placed himself beyond redemption. There was no harbor for him now, and no turning back. Stepping onto the stage, he could feel the heat of the stage lights and hear Janet behind, calling, "Mr. Malters, you can't go out there."

With the resolve of a gun fighter at high noon, he waded onto the stage, where the secretary of Tin Pan Alley was wheeling away his piano. Standing before the cameras, in the split-second before the piano disappeared, he knew he had them. He grabbed the moment as if it were the Olympic torch and appealed to the audience.

"Fellow Mooseketeers, may I have your attention for some urgent news? Mickey's not a moose, but a rat in moose's clothing."

There was no doubt this blasphemy gained the attention of the crowd. Neil continued, "America is not Daisylands. Can't you tell the difference anymore? Malt Daisy's just a tired old man, his grandson's a drug dealer, and your secretary of state is nothing but a thug. All you have to do with these people is believe the exact opposite of everything they say. You think they're looking after you? They control you like sheep. They. Them. In their artificial cocoons, floating around the heavens. They're playing God with your lives. They wouldn't care if South America bombed you all flat. How can you pollute a sewer?"

There was a noticeably stony silence in the amphitheater but for a call from the floor manager. "Script!"

Jimmy appeared from the wings, his pale complexion bristling pink as he recognized the "fruitcake from the hospital." Unable to restrain himself, he marched in front of the cameras.

"What in Christ's name are you saying, boy?" he screamed.

Neil stepped to one side and gestured towards the irate secretary.

"Here he is, folks, the executioner himself. He'll put you all to the wall just to cover his drug debt."

Jimmy was beyond arguing; he came out swinging. Neil ducked and ducked again as Jimmy pursued him around the stage.

"Tell them how you've set yourselves up on Mars, how you used this country to build a haven for yourself, and how now you're going to piss on us."

Jimmy finally connected—a wild roundhouse to the jaw that sent Neil sprawling and a succession of kicks delivered with the viciousness of a street hoodlum. It was then that a long, gangly figure streaked across the stage, flying in on a stage rope and swinging a rail rifle with his spare hand. He collided with Jimmy, who though quick to his feet, was not as fast as the experienced reporter. Neil groaned from the floor.

"Shit, where did you come from?"

"Afternoon zoot." Harvey winked. Then, staring menacingly at the secretary of state, he shouted, "Nobody move. I've killed before."

"Don't fire that thing in here," Jimmy cried urgently. "You'll take the studio with you."

"Shut up!" Harvey screamed, and in the frozen silence of the Moose Hall, a woman's dry voice nagged her husband from the back rows. "Harry, did you lock the Magnobile?"

Harvey commanded, "Now Mr. Secretary, I want a full confession, or I'll use the rifle. Tell us, has the Trans-Daisy Conglomerate been coordinating the trafficking of the narcotic known as Zenine?"

Sweat beaded across the secretary's brow, his face wincing in terror as Harvey lurched the rifle to his shoulder and took aim.

"Yes, yes," he said hastily.

"And have you been using it to lace the national water supply?"

"Yes," he groaned.

Harvey lowered the rifle to his hip as Neil dragged himself to his feet, his ribs aching from several boot marks.

"The only good drug peddler is a dead one," he murmured, echoing the sentiments of the company president. Jimmy dropped to his knees and pleaded, tears pouring from his eyes.

"Don't shoot! I'm only ninety-one years old. I'm to young to die."

Harvey turned and spoke directly to the cameras. It was his chance to add his two cents.

"There, you've heard it from the horse's mouth. These guys aren't politicians; they're gangsters. You can't let them use you anymore. They're not going to get away with it. Do you hear me? We're taking the secretary of state hostage, and don't try to stop us."

There was silence.

"Okay." Harvey motioned to Jimmy with his rifle. "Let's go."

"Wait." Neil ran to the back of the stage and, grabbing Janet's arm as she looked on in astonishment, dragged her out in front of the cameras. "She's coming, too."

She tugged to free herself from Neil's grip as he followed his partner off stage, but he wasn't going to lose her again. The gangly reporter nudged Jimmy with the muzzle of the rifle and marched him past the terrified club members to the stage door.

"Where are we going?" Neil called to him as they walked briskly down the corridor.

"The president's private helipad on the roof. We'll take his jet and make for Canada," Harvey called over his shoulder.

"You'll never get away with it," Jimmy scoffed from his position up front.

Harvey pushed the end of the rifle between his shoulder blades.

"You consider yourself a prisoner of war, Mr. Secretary," he advised. "Remember, we win or lose together."

The end of Harvey's rifle in his back added weight to the argument, and he lead them, as instructed, to the western turret where the president's jet crouched in readiness on the tarmac.

"Get in," Harvey commanded, and they clambered up the gangway.

"Can you fly one of these?" Neil asked as they surveyed the empty cabin.

"No."

"Yes."

Harvey had said no; Janet had said yes.

"Everybody's got their pilot's license, haven't they?" she asked tentatively. Neil and Harvey looked at each other vacantly and then bustled her into the cockpit, making sure Jimmy was in sight. They ordered her to takeoff.

Running her fingers over the instrument panel, she pulled the necessary controls that lifted them from the helipad as gently as a butterfly from a bloom. They hovered for a while as a tumult of journalists and assorted peoples spilled onto the tarmac in pursuit of them. Then, with a final revving of the engines, the jet shot into the darkening sky, leaving those behind on the turret in the billowing exhaust.

11

Nice of Them to Let You Out First

It was a Krudd 7007, a vertical takeoff stratospheric sky plane they were flying in, and Jimmy stood defiantly in the center of the cabin. Harvey faced him, his back to the cockpit, and pointed his gun menacingly.

"You're not going to use that thing in here," Jimmy said. Harvey's eyes told him he wasn't bluffing.

"Just sit over there," he said icily, indicating a long cushioned seat alongside the starboard wall. Neil left Janet at the controls and joined his partner as Jimmy sat down. All three stared at each other until Neil finally broke the silence.

"Well?"

Harvey didn't like taking his attention off Jimmy for too long.

"Well what?" he said.

"Well, I don't know," Neil replied after some consideration.

Harvey was slow to respond, so Jimmy did. "Well don't think this inane little display is going to change anything."

Harvey glared at him.

"I guess that just depends on how important you are to them, doesn't it?" he said.

Jimmy's face paled as he reflected on his position.

"You don't know what you're dealing with," he struggled to say, his mind grappling with the implications. "This is bigger than any one man."

"Bullshit," Neil said. "They all work for you. Take out the king, and it's checkmate."

"But I'm not the king," Jimmy pleaded. "I might be a queen, maybe." He smiled bashfully. "But I'm not the king. That's Malt's job."

"They won't want to lose their queen either," Harvey said grimly, realizing they'd taken the wrong hostage.

Neil laughed sarcastically as Jimmy tried to convince him.

"Listen, you don't know; Zenine costs and this country is bankrupt. This war is just America's way of settling its debt?"

"Bankrupt!" Harvey interrupted hotly. "The Trans-Daisy Conglomerate owns half the universe."

"The company's money is the company's money," Jimmy countered. "America consumes the stuff. America owes for it. We've been keeping the country propped up for years now, waiting until self-sufficiency could be reached by the space colonies. Well, they've done it. America's on its own now. It's about time it woke up."

Harvey was enraged and took aim with the rifle, but Neil deflected the weapon saying he was worth more alive. Jimmy laughed.

"Tell him to pull the trigger," he said. "They're going to blow us out of the sky anyway. We're too hot; they'll waste us all."

He slumped back against the wall as Neil and Harvey eyed each other with the uncomfortable feeling he may know what he was talking about. The air of despondency was broken as Janet slipped from the cockpit and appeared in the cabin.

"So it's true then," she said to Jimmy forlornly. She had overheard everything. Jimmy didn't reply but stared dejectedly into the carpet.

"I don't understand. What's it all been for?"

"You stupid girl," the secretary snapped. "You've never lived on the outside. Why, you ask? So you don't have to live there, that's why. It's all been for you and your children. Somebody's got to keep the torch of civilization burning, even if it is from Mars. Do you want to perish on a dying planet with the rest of them?"

Janet shook her head with despair.

"Let's throw him out of the plane now," Neil suggested.

"No," Janet said. "He might land on a furry animal."

"For God's sake girl," Jimmy said. "There aren't any furry animals left."

"He may be right," Harvey said, ignoring the plight of any organism other than himself. "You know how they deal with terrorists these days.

They shoot first and ask questions later, and it doesn't matter who gets in the way."

"They'll shoot us out of the sky," Jimmy murmured, almost sobbing.

At this moment, a voice from the cockpit urged those aboard the presidential jet to establish contact. Harvey pushed the rail rifle into Neil's hands, instructing Neil to "Keep him covered." Taking Janet's hand, he pulled her into the cockpit. Neil recoiled from the object he found himself so suddenly nursing, but managed to point it more of less at the secretary, who listened keenly for the voice from the control tower.

"Show me how it works," Harvey ordered impatiently. Janet squeezed the microphone into his hand.

"Just press the button when you want to speak."

"This is the presidential jet. Do you read us? Over."

"We read you," the voice replied over the intercom. "State your intentions. Over."

Harvey pressed the button again and, speaking directly to Janet, demanded, "We want a promise of non-hostility toward South America, a government inquiry into the narcotics trafficking, and safe passage for my partner and me guaranteed, over."

"Roger, understood. We have a response. Do you read me? Over," the voice responded.

"Yes, ah, roger," Harvey said nervously.

"You have exactly three minutes to surrender before being vaporized. Over and out."

"What!" Harvey screamed. "Wait, come in. Roger? Wilco! Ian! Anybody?"

Janet shared his alarm, as did Neil and Jimmy.

"Where are we?" Harvey barked.

"We've been circling Washington," Janet said, guilty of procrastinating over setting course for Canada.

"Washington!" Harvey exclaimed. "Parachute! Bail out! Run for cover!" He tried to turn one of his characteristic circles but there wasn't room. "Abandon ship!" he yelled.

"Parachute?" Neil echoed faintly from the cabin.

Janet leapt into the pilot's seat and began throwing levers and pressing buttons, saying, "I can have us down in two."

The plane dropped so suddenly, Neil found himself plastered against the ceiling for a few seconds, as was Jimmy. Harvey fared slightly better, having been warned to hold tight. Jerking to a halt, just inches above Washington Park, Jimmy and Neil crashed to the floor of the cabin.

"Let's get out of here," Harvey ordered while Janet lowered the jet to rest as gently as they had lifted off. They scrambled from the cockpit and, each grabbing one of their stunned confederates, rolled them out the emergency hatch and dragged them clear of the doomed sky plane.

Taking refuge close by behind the corrugated iron and assorted rubbish of a tramps shanty, they had barely caught their breath when a pulse of red flashed into the abandoned aircraft. It glowed briefly with an ethereal sheen before exploding to the point of disintegration. The shanty was flattened by the force of the blast as were others that encircled it. In fact the park was a shanty city in which the presidential jet had crushed a dozen domiciles just by landing.

The shell-shocked aviators, their ears ringing with a high-pitched buzzing noise, gazed at the smoldering mess of devastated hovels. Wary survivors were crawling from the collapsed ruins of shacks, as stunned neighbors looked on. Old men, women, and children, all dressed in rags, wore haggard expressions of morbid curiosity. They were quick to perceive the insiders, in their colorful clothes, as intruders and began to congregate around them.

Harvey still nursed the rail rifle he had the presence of mind to grab as he dragged Neil to the hatch, and the thickening crowd of onlookers maintained a respectful distance as they eyed the weapon. Slowly, the misbegotten terrorists and their hostages rose and dusted themselves off.

"I don't like the look of this," Jimmy said.

"What?" Harvey called through the hiss of his battered eardrum.

Neil heard but wished he hadn't. He'd hoped he had misread the eyes of the gathering crowd. A tall man with a grizzly, greying beard and long, matted hair, looking like the mad monk Rasputin, took a step forward from the circle of park dwellers, but he stopped as Harvey gripped the rifle and brought it to his side.

"Nice gun," he said, looking sternly into Harvey's suspicious eyes.

"What?" Harvey solicited quizzically.

Neil would have prompted, but he wasn't sure he'd caught that himself, the blast had temporarily deafened him, too.

"Something about having fun," Jimmy bellowed.

"Fun?" Harvey exclaimed.

"No, I said 'gun,'" the man repeated. He could see they still hadn't heard so he shouted. "I said 'gun.' It's a nice gun."

"Oh," Harvey grunted in comprehension. "Yeah, it's okay. Do you have one?"

"No," the bearded man replied slowly, shaking his head.

"Good," Harvey said, and maintained his grip on the trigger. The bearded man looked agitated and spat his frustration out onto the ground by his feet.

"Now I don't mean to be unneighborly, pardner, but you've just parked your flying machine on my house."

Harvey looked blankly at Neil.

"It was his house," Neil shouted, pointing.

"Oh, oh," Harvey murmured.

Janet gazed skyward. "So give me a ticket," she said flippantly. The man was silent for a while and found it in himself to spit again.

"Do you know who we are?" Harvey asked meaningfully.

"You're insiders, aren't you?" the man stated.

"We've just come from the Mickey Moose Club," Harvey told him in an effort to impress.

The man looked around at his brethren who murmured amongst themselves. He turned back to Harvey. "Well whoopee," he said flatly.

A distraught woman emerged from the circle and stepped to the bearded man's side.

"That was old Michael O'Tyson who lived in that shack over there," she sobbed, pointing to the charred remains. "Poor old Mick, he went to bed early; may he rest in peace. Wouldn't have hurt a soul, but now look."

The murmurs amongst the crowd grew, and so did the unease of the four intruders.

"We're very sorry; we didn't mean to land. We were sort of shot down," Neil volunteered in an attempt to placate them.

"Nice of them to let you out first, wasn't it?" a voice from the crowd heckled as the murmurs grew to jeers.

"No, listen," Neil shouted above the growing cacophony. "We've just escaped from Fantasy Castle. We've taken the leader of the international drugs cartel, Jimmy, your secretary of state, as a hostage. We want to stop the war."

"Sounds downright un-American to me." A short African American, built like a battle tank, stepped to the other side of the tall, bearded man, who spat again. The crowd grumbled with agreement.

"It's typical of you insiders. You land in the middle of our village. You don't care who gets in the way. You feed us bullshit about kings and castles. You threaten us with your guns. You're full of crap." This speech by the tall bearded man incited the passions of the brooding park dwellers, who shouted their demands for justice between long and venomous insults.

"Let's burn 'em," the short man said.

"Wait, you don't understand," Neil pleaded. "We're on your side."

"Put down that rifle and say that," the tall man said.

Harvey glanced at Neil, but it was Jimmy who advised, "Don't you dare."

The short man took a step forward. Harvey tensed and aimed the rifle in his direction.

"I'll shoot!" he screamed, and compelled by his own sense of panic, fired the gun above the heads of his adversaries in a display of resolve. On the far side of the park, a grand old building from the early twentieth century exploded with spectacular immediacy and collapsed. Fourteen stories of tumbling masonry blew a cloud of choking black dust into the surrounding streets.

"Holy hell!" Neil gasped as the filtering extremities of the dust cloud settled like falling snow around them. The circle of onlookers dove to the ground, leaving the four intruders and three outspoken park dwellers standing, facing each other resolutely.

"Hey Jaco, wanna go play some handball?" the tall man whispered, as the last falling brick came to rest. His companion made no reply.

Harvey, suddenly realizing the full and awesome potential of the weapon he held, dropped it. Jimmy was quick. It was on the ground only a few seconds before he whipped it up and spun around to threaten the cautiously rising crowd. They fell backward over themselves in an effort to retreat as the secretary spun again and faced those in the circle's center.

"Janet, come over here," he ordered.

But Janet didn't move. She burst into tears instead, crying, "Who said there aren't any furry animals left?"

Jimmy rolled his eyes to the heavens and sighed.

"I'll make a deal with you," he said, speaking directly to the park dwellers. "You can burn the others, but I'm walking out of here. Janet, come over here."

Janet raised her eyes, wet with tears that streaked her face, and sobbed, "You're a crook Jimmy. When we get back, I'll have your Mooseketeer antlers."

Jimmy's patience was short at the best of times, and these were not the best of times. On the brink of shooting his way out, the relentless drone of an approaching squadron of police choppers stopped him. Their searchlights pin-holed the park and zeroed in on the disintegrated jet. Detecting the presence of an armory, they targeted the rail rifle and took it out with a pulse-laser. Jimmy exploded like the sky plane before him, and in the frozen silence that followed, the booming command from the police loudspeaker was deafening. *"Nobody move!"*

Whereupon the entire park erupted in a wild stampede.

Grabbing Janet by the arm, Neil ran with Harvey to the park's perimeter, as the choppers hovered and giant holographic images of Mickey Moose and his hunting dog, Plato, stamped through the shadows behind them. With columns of troopers snaking their way through the streets of the old city, the only escape was down through the lower floors of the nearest building, into the basement and beyond. Running deeper down, further in, over the countless beddings of vagrants who called it home, they fled until the floors were just rock and eventually the walls and ceilings were as well. Deeper down, further in, their passage was lit only by the crude pitch torches they lifted from the basement dormitories. They marched on until, exhausted, they dropped their tired bodies to the damp rocky floor and caught their breath.

12

It's What You Call Derwinism

AS THEIR PANTING SUBSIDED IN the deafening silence of the cavern, a distant mumble danced on the edges of their imaginations, and a deadly odor haunted their nostrils. Harvey went to investigate. A wild scream brought Neil, with Janet close behind, running through a series of stony antechambers and into a cave alive with firelight. Trapped against the rock wall by a strange, furry beast that growled like a canine at its cornered prey, Harvey was covering his eyes with his hands and cowering. Beside him, a short, stocky creature in blue overalls held a burning torch to his face. Its black eyes glistened from inside blacker, baggy rings that encircled them and bulged slightly as they struggled to see through the flickering of the fire. Its face was otherwise indiscernible beneath a mane of sooty black hair, which seemed to radiate in all directions from every part of its head. The overall effect gave it the appearance of a walking chimney brush.

Neil was horrified, and Janet fainted when a bland, toneless voice, sounding like the operator of the international telephone exchange, drawled from behind.

"You were rarght, Ralph. there 'er more of 'em."

What stood behind them was a ghastly spectacle—a creature, tall by comparison to the other and skinnier than the overalls that hung so loosely on its weedy body. It was bald, and its broad, flat nose protruded from two black rings around its large, bulging eyes. Its lips were a paradox—the top one thin, the bottom bulbous—and they were set wide across its reclining chin.

"Must be a convention or somethin'," it concluded.

"Mort!" the short, hairy one rasped. "What would dey be doin' convenin' down here?"

"I dunno," the skinny one retorted, "but it sure would be convenin' if they got back to it. I done thang we got grub for six."

Harvey peeked from behind his hands.

"Neil, is that you?" he asked hopefully.

Neil wasn't sure, by this stage, exactly who he was, and he was irritated to be reminded of a detail that seemed irrelevant given their present predicament. "Goddamn!" he shouted. "I don't know."

"They's not underworlders, nup," Mort droned behind him. "They's topsiders, sure."

Neil spun to face him. "Outsiders!" he shrieked, as if this correction somehow justified their presence.

"Hey," Harvey cried, "I don't want to interrupt, but do you want to call your dog off?"

The furry beast rose on its hind legs and leaned its forelegs on its hips.

"Hey, who you call a dog a your face?" it said in a thick Neapolitan accent. Harvey stared, unsure whether to be relieved or to panic.

"Allow me to introduce you," the short hairy one said congenially. "Dis here is Komo."

Komo dropped back on all fours and scrambled to the creature's side. "Komo's been gettin' around da tunnels down here so long, he just feels more comfortable on his hands."

"Yeah," Komo spoke for himself. "It's a what you a call a Derwinism. Adapt an' a survive."

"Komo can get anywhere," Mort boasted for his friend. "I'd never get into some of the places he gets to."

"Anyway," Komo added. "You stand up, and all a the blood a falls from your brain. You get a dopey."

The creatures suddenly seemed less threatening, though Harvey found it hard to believe the furry beast was human. He could see him clearer in the firelight. Except for his grubby knee-length shorts and the top of his head, where his hair was extremely thin, he was covered from his beard to his toes in a thick mat of dark hair. He was squatting on his legs, and Harvey had to resist the impulses to go over and pat him on the head. He looked meekly over to the creature, even hairier, holding the torch.

"And I'm Ralph," it said. "Dis is Mort."

77

"We're identical twins." Mort wheezed between a proud smile.

Neil looked blankly from one to the other. Mort slouched into his nuggetty skinniness, and Ralph bursting defiantly through his chimney brush head.

"But you don't look anything like each other," he commented.

"Just because you look different, it don't mean you're not the same," Mort told him.

"Oh my God! Janet!" Harvey, having just noticed her lying at Neil's feet, rushed to her side.

Propping her in front of the fire, Neil lightly patted her cheeks till she regained consciousness. But when she saw the five pairs of eyes shinning in the firelight, she screamed and passed out again. When she came to, she was gently introduced to Komo and the identical twins, to which she replied, "But they don't look anything like each other."

She was then offered a bowl of stew. She couldn't see the bowl's contents clearly in the dull light, but nothing could disguise the smell—thick and strong as the six o'clock feed at the animal shelter—which threatened, as it swilled sluggishly in the smooth, plastic bowl, to taste even stronger.

"You don't expect me to eat this," she said indignantly, throwing aside all pretense of good manners.

Ralph beamed at her through his baggy black rings. "Rat stew," he told her. "Mort's specialty."

Just inches from his mouth, Neil dropped his spoon and fought to suppress his rising stomach.

"We're on a trappin' expedition," Ralph explained. "Rats for d' fines' tables in d' underworld. It's our motto. 'We trap 'em, you eat 'em.'"

It was too much for Harvey. He had to run to the next cave for a discrete chunder before returning sheepishly to the campfire. As he sat down, Neil was explaining to their hosts why they should be concerned about Malter Daisy Jr. and his diabolical plans.

"It's really very simple," he was saying. "The insiders have been sedating the outsiders with narcotics from the southsiders and poisoning the water, which is drunk by the underworlders. This is all so some of the topsiders, that is to say the insiders, can become otherworlders and dump on all of us."

He looked keenly from Mort to Ralph to see if his words had made any impression, but he received only bewildered expressions of non-comprehension.

Hearing Neil clarify the issue as effectively as using a bag of dirt to clean clothes, Harvey interrupted, "The point is that someone's been poisoning the water with an addictive substance called Zenine. They've hooked the entire country, and we're going to war because of it."

He looked to see if he had helped, but Mort looked at him as if he'd delivered the punch line of a bad joke.

"Aw!" he said. "We don't drink that water, we've known about that fer years." Now it was Neil and Harvey's turn to be confused.

"We drink from mineral springs untapped by the topsiders."

"You've known?" Harvey could not contain his surprise.

"Sure," Mort replied. "We go to ever' part of the city from down here. Why we could hear gov'ment meetings if we wanted. We have done, but we don' bother with it none. It don' make much difference to us no how."

"You can get into Fantasy Castle from down here?" Neil was as amazed as Harvey.

"Komo once watched President Daisy take a bath," Mort said proudly.

"Why sure," Ralph added. "Dere's a network of tunnels dat stretches from coast to coast. It's a miracle of primitive engineering."

Janet had decided Komo, a very furry animal indeed, was not nearly as ferocious as she had presumed and was scratching his stomach vigorously as he writhed on the floor in ecstasy, his paws hanging limply in the air. She beamed a large smile, as if to say, *Isn't he cute?* But she gave no sign she had even heard Mort's statement about the matrix of tunnels connecting them to Fantasy Castle.

"Could you get us inside the castle?" Harvey was getting excited.

"To the president's bathroom," Mort confirmed smugly.

Harvey had an idea and looked to Neil to see if he was thinking the same thing. "We might as well take this to the top," he said.

Harvey had become very quickly convinced that the only hope of saving their own and the country's deteriorating situation lay in a direct confrontation with the president himself. Neil was understandably cautious, but he could think of no practical alternative, and Janet, who had been brought up in the castle by her fabulously wealthy parents, both of whom occupied high government positions, would be keen to get home, even if it was by way of a subterranean thoroughfare in the bowels of the underworld.

"Ralph, would you take us there now?" Harvey asked candidly.

And this was when the bewildered overworlders learned that the identical twins, had diverging views on just about every issue save one, that they were identical twins. They took the opposing corner in any dispute, and Harvey's request produced a typically longwinded debate over whether or not to oblige. Ralph, an energetic and charitable soul, whose greatest satisfaction was to help make life easier for others, was keen to take them. Mort on the other hand, morose and lazy, thought the castle was boring and wanted to take their guests to the Emerald Caves instead. Eventually, they resorted to the method they always used when both parties remained intractable on a given subject.

"The democracy coins," Mort droned as forcefully as he could. "Fetch the democracy coins."

"Fetch?" Komo's ears picked up.

"Yeah, d' democracy coins." Ralph agreed.

The overworlders blinked at each other as Komo ran in several Harvey-like circles, scampered over to a pile of sacks by the wall, and returned with a small rat-hide pouch. He handed it to Ralph, who reached inside and withdrew three shinny coins, which he then distributed, one each, to Mort and Komo.

"Okay," he said. "In da spirit of true democracy, we agree to stand by da decision of da call."

Mort and Komo nodded, lips wet.

"Then heads we take dem to da castle, tails we go to da Emerald Caves."

"If it's all the same to you, I'd just like to go to the surface," Janet interjected timidly. Ralph didn't hear her.

"Okay?" he repeated. The others nodded again, their large eyes bulging excitedly from their uniformly baggy rings.

"Toss!" Mort screamed. Neil and Janet jumped, Harvey cringed, and the coins were sent spinning into the air. Six eager pairs of eyes followed them to the floor where they glinted their decision in the firelight, two heads and a tail.

"Da castle it is," Ralph said, and Harvey cheered.

13

They Don't Have Horses
on the Moon

IT WAS A LONG JOURNEY to the castle, and Mort and Ralph advised going back to their cave at the trading post before setting out. Even this destination was some distance away, and all were in need of rest by the time they arrived. Mort and Ralph's catch of rats was bartered at the trading post for pitch and wood for their torches, a large clay flask of Hades Hooch (a distilled alcoholic beverage of such potency it caused the uninitiated to pass out just by holding the bottle), and various sundry items such as banjo strings for Mort's ukulele. With these provisions accounted for, the trappers retired to their den among the caves of a subterranean city hidden deep beneath old Washington.

Hungry though they were, the three overworlders were asleep before Ralph had lit the burner to prepare their meal. Mort was already stringing his ukulele while humming his favorite drinking song as an overture, and Komo was skinning a large rat for the skillet. Within half an hour, dinner was sizzling in the pan, Mort was yodeling a tuneful underworld ballad through Neil's intermittent snoring, and the cold, stone walls of the den had taken on a cozy, domestic serenity.

When Neil awoke many hours later, Mort and Ralph were asleep, and Janet was playing fetch with Komo while Harvey stoked the fire back to life.

"You're up," Harvey said, returning to his seat on a long log bench. Neil gazed blankly around the cave, remembered where he was, and felt extremely down. He shook his head.

"Cheer up," Harvey said. Janet sat beside him and tossed the fetching stick into the fire. Komo almost leapt in after it, but decided the game was over and lay down at her feet instead.

"Well, at least we've still got one hostage," Harvey continued, trying to be positive.

"Hostage!" Neil shouted softly, taking a seat on the log. "She's not a hostage."

Alarmed to be thought of as their prisoner, Janet edged closer to Neil for support. Harvey looked surprised.

"Well if she's not a hostage," he asked, genuinely curious, "what's she doing here?"

Now Neil was surprised, forgetting he hadn't introduced them.

"Harvey, this is the woman I love," he said.

If Janet was alarmed before, she was horrified now and instinctively moved over next to Harvey.

"Do you want to run that by me again?" Harvey said blandly.

"She's not a hostage," Neil repeated, embarrassed by such a personal admission, and adding, as if to clarify the situation, "this is my wife."

It was Harvey's turn to shake his head.

"Helen's not going to like this," he said.

"This is Helen!" Neil said loudly, in the hope extra volume could make Harvey understand. The perplexed cameraperson had been worried about his partner, but now he knew he was crazy.

"Are you in love with this guy?" Harvey asked Janet, as if that was obviously impossible.

"Love!" Janet gagged, as a cynical laugh exploded from her lips. "You drag me at gunpoint from the most important club meeting this century, have me almost shot out of the sky while stealing the president's sky plane, cause me to nearly be burned alive in the Washington Ghetto, send me running from our own security forces into an underground hell I didn't even know existed, then make me a collaborator in a planned assault on the president's bathroom. I'm cold. I'm hungry. My feet are killing me. At this moment, I'd murder my own grandmother, and you ask me if I love him!"

Sarcasm was wasted on the secretary for small, furry animals. It was wasted on Harvey too.

"Was that a no or a yes?" he questioned her.

Janet bit her lip and held her breath, releasing air slowly as she seethed, "That was a no." Having succeeded in controlling her impatience, she threw it all away and screamed, "And I hope you both die a horrible death at the hands of some baggy-eyed monster and have your rotting carcasses gnawed on by a herd of carnivorous rodents, until the only thing left is a pile of decomposing rat shit in the bottom of one of Mort's traps."

Harvey looked to his partner and back to Janet.

"Okay, okay; you're not a hostage," he said. "Sheesh."

They both looked over to Neil, who really didn't care anymore.

"Okay, and I don't love you," he conceded, crossing his fingers.

Unsure if this derision qualified as an apology, Janet raised her nose ungraciously in the air and looked away.

"Oh, my achin' head," Mort groaned while sitting up in his bed, his brain pounding from a hooch-inspired hangover.

"What's all da commotion?" Ralph called, sitting up beside him.

"Mornin'!" Harvey greeted them. "Just getting ready to meet the president."

It was a good eight-hour trek to the castle and an arduous journey for the inexperienced overworlders. Having only stopped briefly to rest, they were quite breathless by the time Ralph announced they had arrived.

With a rope clamped firmly between his teeth, Komo scrambled onto Ralph's shoulders, and in a nimble gymnastic display, he balanced carefully for a while before easing his torso into one of the vertical drains that pierced the ceiling. One by one, the others climbed the rope after him and found themselves standing in a vast concrete chamber with a steel staircase bolted to the wall.

"Dis way," Ralph ordered and led them up the stairs and through a jungle of corridors and cold concrete rooms. They reached the basement air-conditioning plant without seeing a soul, and from there, they continued their penetration by moving up staircases and scaffolding, which serviced the wide arteries of the cooling ducts. Mort knew his way around the castle like the back of his hand. Like Janet, he had been raised in the castle, but he came from the other side of the walls.

They finally reached a steel mesh recess that boasted a doorway to the Daisy level of the inner castle. Once through this door, they were vulnerable to detection. At one stage, they passed a team of technicians repairing silicon cells in one of the domestic computer rooms, but they were mistaken for eccentric relatives of the first family. Soon Ralph had them crawling again through the just-wide-enough ducts of the air-conditioning for the president's private residence.

"Look a here," Komo directed and then squeezed against the duct wall so Harvey behind him could see. Through the small grate in the duct casing ahead, he could see why Komo was so excited. It was the president's bathroom, landscaped in gold and silver with palms and ferns in marble pots, fountains trickling in lazy waterfalls, and statuettes of Greek heroes posing in various alcoves. There were twin hand basins, twin baths, and twin toilets. Mort's voice could be heard from somewhere ahead.

"Well, now you've seen the bathroom, do you want to go to the Emerald Caves?"

"We want to see the president, not his bathroom," Harvey shouted, as if Mort were too stupid to be believed. Mort certainly appeared to be stupid, especially with a few hooches under his belt, but he was, in fact, in possession of an IQ approaching genius and was merely being sarcastic. His brother—who, by virtue of his more forceful personality, acted as commander-in-chief of their trapping operation—was by comparison pretty dumb. And Komo, despite a certain natural cunning, had the mental capacity of a village idiot.

"You want to see da president?" It was Ralph's voice. "He's in here."

Neil was closest and edged his face against the grate. What he could see inside was a large room, dimly lit, that housed all the trappings of a master bedroom: closets, bureaus, a vanity table, a few assorted extras such as the adjacent lounge facilities, a bar, a mirrored ceiling, and of course, a king-size bed. There was someone sleeping in it.

Silently, Ralph's experienced fingers prized the grate from the duct wall. Easing himself through the opening, he dropped to the thickly carpeted floor. The others followed, and soon all were assembled at the end of the bed, peering with a cautious but curious reverence at the sleeping figure. With his grey hair and thin grey moustache, this was the man who had created Daisylands, made a thousand movies, and spawned an empire. It was the president of the United States, Malt Daisy.

As if subconsciously alerted to the six pairs of eyes that stared at him, he stirred, tossed his head from side to side, and appeared to be battling to wake himself. The intruders looked at each other anxiously. No one was familiar with the correct procedure for barging in and waking a president unannounced.

He opened his eyes, lifted his head, saw the strange band of intruders at the end of the bed, and screamed. Then he hid quickly under the covers. The sound of footsteps resonated from behind the walls, and as if by reflex, the intruders scattered. Neil, Harvey, and Janet leapt under the bed as Mort and Ralph disappeared into closets. Komo found time to run several desperate circles before leaping back into the air-conditioning duct just as the door slid open and two men hurried to the president's side.

"Mr. President!" one exclaimed.

"Everything all right, Malt?" the other asked.

The old man peered out from under the sheets. The apparitions were gone, and with only his doctor and Elwin, his minder, there, he felt it was safe to reemerge from the protection of the blankets.

"Ghosts, monsters," he garbled and pointed to the end of the bed.

"There, there," the doctor said, "it's just a bad dream."

Neil thought the voice sounded familiar.

"You shouldn't eat so much before you go to bed," the minder said, his prize-fighter's physique fighting to free itself from a suit that was a size too small. "Shit, the old bastard's hallucinating," he added under his breath.

"More medication," the doctor commanded.

"More!" Elwin cried. "I think he's had enough."

"Not more medication," Malt whined. "That's all you give me. If I've eaten too much before retiring, it's because I'm full of your damn medication."

"Now, now," the doctor said, pressing him back into the pillows, "don't go on so much."

He produced a pill from his pocket and poured a glass of water from a jug on the bureau, but Malt resisted as it was pushed into his mouth.

"Cut it out, Barnyard, just put it over there, and I'll have it in a minute."

Neil knew he'd recognized that voice.

"I think you should take it straight away," Barnyard urged.

85

"But they're haunting me," Malt complained.

"Who's haunting you?" Barnyard jeered. "You've had a bad dream. Just relax, and it will all be better by morning."

"You're the bad dream," Malt said sarcastically. "You're a goddamn nightmare."

"Yes, it's not easy being 157 years old, is it?" Barnyard patronized him. "Now be a good president and take your medication; you've got a big day ahead of you. You have to be fresh for your speech tomorrow. After all, it's not every day you get to declare war on a billion people."

"The speech, yes," Malt mumbled. "It's that speech that's giving me nightmares. I'm all right—just a bad dream. Thank you; you can go now."

The two men nodded at each other and retreated slyly through the open door, with a final instruction shouted before it snapped shut behind them. "Don't forget to take your medication."

All was quiet for a while, no sound from the president's bed, and in due course, the intruders sneaked out from their hiding places and again congregated at the end of the bed. Harvey led Janet to the president's side and whispered, "Wake him up."

She had come to see the president as something of a father figure, her own parents being a lesbian couple, and he embodied the image of the patriarch she had never known. Tentatively, she placed a hand on the old man's shoulder and shook him gently.

He jerked to a sitting position.

"Janet!" he cried, trembling as he recognized her.

"Hello, Mr. President," she said, with a cheery smile that disguised her nervousness.

"You're, you're dead."

Janet cast a quick glance at Neil and the underworlders at the end of the bed.

"If only," she grumbled.

"You died in a plane crash," Malt said. He couldn't believe his eyes. "They said you were dead."

Only twenty-four hours before, he had been informed of the destruction of his sky plane and the deaths of all those on board. Like Neil, he too had woken to a strange new century and had witnessed and experienced many strange events. Though he had never believed in ghosts, demons, Satan, Jesus Christ, or even the Pilgrim Fathers, he was now prepared to believe anything—even that he was being haunted.

"No, Mr. President," Harvey spoke. "We didn't die."

"Who, who are you?" Malt gasped, and Neil came round to the side of the bed and stood beside Janet.

"We're reporters for the *Los Angeles Tribune*," he said.

"What! That rag of a news disc!" Malt scoffed. "That biased, sensational, typically scurrilous example of the popular press!"

"Who told you that?" Harvey asked, proud of his publication and hurt to hear it so comprehensively vilified.

"I saw it on a news disc," Malt replied, looking down at the underworlders, who smiled benignly at their president from the end of the bed. They didn't have much respect for overworlders, but they held a reverence for the office and the man who held it. They were duly humbled.

"What do you funny-looking people think you're doing here?" Malt demanded, his shock and confusion hiding behind a bluster of trespassed indignation.

"We, er, ah," Ralph stammered sheepishly.

"You've got a beautiful bathroom." Mort wheezed from behind a congenial smile, a smile he put on when he was on his best behavior. Malt turned back to the secretary for small, furry animals.

"Janet, what's happening? Reporters. Demons. Tell me you're not dead."

"I'm not dead, Mr. President," Janet told him forcefully, and with more than a hint of impatience in her voice, she added, "We escaped. I'm alive; we're all alive."

She cocked an eyebrow at the underworlders and shuddered.

"Alive!" Malt exclaimed, and his dismay dissipated as he perceived a tangible threat from the two men. "You guys. You're the guys who broke up the meeting."

He looked frightened, and Harvey braced himself, ready to gag his mouth if he screamed.

"Oh, Mr. President." Janet dropped to her knees, bursting into a shower of tears that dissolved the old man's urgency to scream. "Something terrible has happened, and you must know about it."

"Something terrible?" Malt echoed.

"Yes," she blubbered. "There's been a cover up. They've been telling us lies, but it's all true."

"Please hear her out," Neil said when Malt fidgeted and looked up with bewilderment.

"Mr. President, there aren't any furry animals left."

"Huh?" Harvey grunted. Malt looked surprised then angry.

"You expect me to believe this?" he gasped. Janet wept openly and Neil stared absently at the ceiling; he'd hoped to avoid this aspect of the indictment.

"If this is true," Malt stated, "then I'm deeply distressed; yes, I am. It's a scandal, and we'll do everything we can to go out there and get them back. Yes, we will."

He was using his most statesmanlike voice.

"You can't get them back," Harvey argued. "Don't you understand? They're gone. You insiders are all the same. What would you know or care? They don't have horses on the moon."

Malt seemed genuinely troubled as he stroked Janet's head in sympathy.

"I don't know what this world has come to," he whispered sadly.

"Mr. President, there's more," Neil said.

"More?" He looked so helpless in his laced nightshirt.

"There is a conspiracy against the country by the Trans-Daisy Conglomerate," Neil told him. "They've been using you to front a government that is a smoke screen for their operations. They're trafficking in narcotics, and they are the orchestrators of this war we're about to be hurled into."

"No, no," the old man said. "You're terrorists. Where's Jimmy? Where's the secretary of state?"

It was all too much for the old man to cope with; he could only handle one tragedy at a time.

"Jimmy's dead," Janet wailed. "Our own choppers shot him dead."

Malt was obviously dazed and shook his head.

"Jimmy dead. Where's Malter? He'll fix it."

Harvey could see the old man was having difficulty accepting these accusations, and in an attempt to convince him, he strode to the holovision unit and slipped in his camera's memory card of their interview with Malter Jr.

"Watch this," he said, and they did, beginning with Neil's introduction in the foyer of Malter Jr.'s apartments. Though much was filmed from the seat upon which Harvey laid the camera—thus only showing Malter's face when he sat down, and other times, just his crotch and the seat of Neil's and Harvey's pants—the soundtrack made compelling listening. At its end, Malt leaned back with resignation, his resistance beaten, his spirit sapped. He believed them now; he'd seen it on holovision.

"Sir," Harvey summated, "we can't let this happen. There has to be a way we can stop them. You're the president; do something!"

Malt was the president. He'd been president for ten years, and in that time, he had been shuttled between the hospital and endless rehearsals for the monthly Moose Club meetings. There had been little time for him to familiarize himself with the new world he'd been reborn into, but he had accepted it keenly in his initial enthusiasm for his miraculous resuscitation. However, ten frenetic years of learning what he could about the new century had left him with an inner sadness when he remembered the simpler world of his previous existence. He never could shake the nagging thought that we are each comfortable in the time frame we are born into and no other. These feelings had given rise to a suspicion about the country he now presided over and impatience with the excessive medical attention lavished upon him.

He had come to know and trust Janet during the many club meetings they had attended. Her startling news struck a chord in him that seemed to justify his growing disenchantment with the twenty-first century. But he was an old man, and at times like this, he felt it.

"But what can I do?" he said dejectedly. "Jimmy writes all the scripts."

"Jimmy's dead," Harvey reaffirmed. "It's time you did a bit of script writing."

Malt's face brightened. "Yes," he said, reinvigorated. "Just like in the beginning. I'll write the scripts." He thought for a moment. "But what shall I write?"

Harvey exchanged glances with Neil. There was a twinkle in his eye, and Janet stopped sobbing and looked up hopefully.

"Well to begin with," Neil considered, "why not write war out of the script? Write in appeasement instead. That's a beginning."

"And stop lacing the water supply with drugs," Harvey added. "What about a national detoxification program? Everybody out there is tripping off their faces. Let's get real; this country's got to go cold Botswanian Ostrich."

"And make it illegal to eat furry animals," Janet said.

"What?" Mort interjected suddenly from the end of the bed. "You can't do that. What about our traps?"

This interruption caught Janet by surprise, but she dismissed Mort's concerns by assuring him quickly that rats didn't count.

"Yeah," Malt said as he deliberated on the possibilities. "And we can outlaw cryogenics."

"We can outlaw the whole Trans-Daisy Conglomerate," Harvey said victoriously.

"Oh no," Malt moaned and drew a very long face. "Malter's not going to like this."

"Tell him to go take a running jump," Neil said flippantly.

"Tell him yourself," came Malt's reply. "He's in the next room."

Harvey raised his eyebrows.

"What's he doing here?" He exclaimed. "He hasn't set foot on Earth for seven years."

"That's right," Malt said. "But when you guys kidnapped Jimmy, he flew straight down here to take charge."

"But you're the president," Neil said, indignant that a representative of the people should have his due authority so usurped.

"Yes, but . . ." Malt floundered. "But I don't actually run anything. I mean, I do what a president does. You know? I chair the Mickey Moose Club, make speeches, attend luncheons, eat shrimp and caviar, and play golf, that sort of thing. I don't actually run anything."

"Well you're going to start running things," Neil said. "They haven't changed the Constitution have they?"

"What Constitution?" Harvey asked.

"No, you boys don't understand," Malt pleaded. "I'm out of place here. I don't belong in this world. I don't understand it. Too much has happened. I don't know what's going on anymore."

Harvey could see the old man sinking into despair, a luxury he was determined not to allow him.

"Look," he said, "between all of us, we represent the major regions of the country, inside, outside, and under. You need a new Cabinet, some good advisors. Think of us as your counsel. You need a new secretary of state—appoint Janet, she's qualified."

"Me?" Janet was caught off-guard, but Malt looked receptively thoughtful. Neil was developing a great sympathy for the old man. He felt he somehow held the key to the dilemma of his own projection into this strange new century.

"Mr. President," he said, "I'm not from this time either."

Malter gazed blankly at him.

"Oh no," Harvey mumbled. Neil could feel his partner's disapproval but continued anyway. There was a connection with this fellow time traveler he wanted to discover.

"Mr. President, I came from the twentieth century like yourself. I woke at Daisylands the day I met you there. This is not my place either." He stopped, thoughtful about what he was really trying to say. All that came to mind was, "I want to go back!"

Malt eyed him cautiously. Was it possible Neil had been resuscitated from a hibernation capsule like he had been? He responded sympathetically, as if Neil were a fellow American he stumbled over while lost in an African jungle.

"You want to go back?" he said softly. "It's a funny thing about traveling in time. It would appear it is possible to go forward, but you can never go back. It's an irreversible law of the universe."

He sighed, and Neil felt suddenly heavy, as if his soul had sunk, like a stone in the ocean.

"You can discuss the last century later," Harvey said impatiently. "Right now there's work to be done. Did you say you were making a speech tomorrow, declaring war?"

Malt nodded.

"You can't make that speech, Mr. President."

"But I've got to," Malt pleaded. "It's in the script."

"Screw the script," Neil shouted emotionally. "Throw the script away. We're writing the script now, remember?"

"But what will I write?" Malt despaired.

Neil and Harvey looked at each other.

"He's not listening," Neil said.

Harvey was prepared to be patient and outline a revision of the impending speech, but he was interrupted by the sound of the door sliding open. It was a large room and the bed was not visible from the doorway, positioned as it was around a slight corner. The intruders froze for a second and exchanged frightened glances as a voice inquired, "Is everything all right in there, Mr. President?"

A mad scramble ensued as all six of them dove under the bed. The closets and air-conditioning vent were dangerously exposed to the open doorway. Mort and Ralph somehow managed to squeeze in between the overworlders, even though noses were uncomfortably pressed into foreign armpits and various limbs jabbed various bodies in unforgiving places. But room for Komo there was not, and he was left scampering from one side of the bed to the other in search of an opening as Elwin crept in.

"Ah ha!" the minder exclaimed, as he saw Komo running on all fours in desperate circles at the end of the bed, and Malt grimacing furtively. "I thought I heard voices. Malt, what's he doing here?"

"Ah, er," Malt faltered.

"Who is he?" Elwin asked. "What is he?"

"A woof?" Komo volunteered hopefully.

Elwin looked unconvinced, and Malt stared at the creature, unsure of what to make of him himself. Elwin looked closer, and as an expression of repulsion stretched across his pummeled face, he muttered, "Jesus, I thought we'd had this place sprayed."

"A meow?" Komo tried, aware some people didn't like dogs.

"Well whoever you are, whatever you are, you're going." Elwin decided.

He was about to forcibly eject the intruder when Malt shouted, "No, I want to keep him! If you want to throw something out, throw yourself out."

"You can't keep him," Elwin said. "You don't *keep* people."

Malt took a closer look at the four-footed beast whimpering on the floor. "You mean it's human?"

"I don't know what it is, but it's going," Elwin answered.

"No," Malt insisted. "I found him, and he's mine. Don't touch him, or I'll scream." As Elwin advanced upon the cringing Komo, Malt began to bellow for his doctor. The minder was not dissuaded by this and grappled gamely with the hairy creature, who proved to be exceedingly difficult to seize hold of. The commotion was such that Dr. Barnyard came quickly, but by the time he arrived, a defeated Elwin was sitting, legs outstretched on the floor and Komo had somehow perched himself in a position of safety atop one of the closets.

"What the hell's going on here?" Barnyard barked. "Elwin, what are you doing on the floor? It's your turn to deal."

"Forget the game," Elwin told him. "Go get Mr. Daisy."

"Don't be stupid; I'm not waking Mr. Daisy," Barnyard protested.

"Barnyard," Malt ordered. "Tell that simpleton to leave my pet alone."

"Pet?" Barnyard retorted. "What pet?"

"He means that thing," Elwin said, pointing to the top of the closet.

"Holy moose shit!" Barnyard murmured. "What the hell is that?"

"It's mine," Malt said. "Just leave it alone and clear out."

The doctor eyed Elwin, who picked himself up off the floor and straightened the elastic band that circled his collar and held up his tie.

"I'll get Mr. Daisy," the doctor said, understanding the reason for Elwin's request. He departed quickly as the minder stood vigil beside the president.

"Just where did you find him?" he asked suspiciously.

"What's it to you?" Malt spat at him.

"He might be an assassin," Elwin said, as if this justified his concern. He was, after all, the president's personal bodyguard, amongst other things.

"Where's the gun?" Malt volleyed, totally unsympathetic to Elwin's professional obligations.

"Maybe he's going to eat you," the minder returned sarcastically, staring with disbelief at the cowering underworlder.

"Yeah, maybe he's hungry," Malt said. "Elwin, make yourself useful and go get him a bone or something."

Elwin's mind immediately thought *bait,* and he smiled evilly as Barnyard returned with Malter Jr. They strode to the side of the bed—Malter was still tying the cord of his bathrobe—and Barnyard pointed to Komo, who winced at them from his vantage point on the closet.

"What's going on, Granddad," Malter snapped.

"This moron's trying to take my pet away," Malt said, glaring at Elwin. "Tell him to mind his own business."

"But, Granddad, minding you is his business," Malter reminded him.

"Now don't get cocky with me, you young whipper-snapper," Malt scolded.

"I'm 104 years old, Granddad," Malter responded dryly "Now let's have no more of this nonsense. What is that thing up there, and where did you get it from?"

"It's my pet," Malt said. "I found him, and I'm going to keep him. I'm going to keep all of them."

Under the bed, Harvey and Neil groaned, Neil because he realized the old man had just given away the fact that they were hiding, and Harvey because of the fart Mort elicited, a legacy of his rat stew.

"All of whom?" Malter asked, eyeing the old man suspiciously as his nostrils flinched instinctively from the slowly rising aroma.

There was a short and smelly silence as Malt tried to collect his thoughts and then replied, "All those people who are hiding under the bed."

"Aw shit," came Harvey's muted expletive from beneath the mattress.

Malter looked at Elwin with an expression that would have melted titanium.

"You're meant to be minding him," he said. "Just how many people, things, have you let in here?"

"None boss, honest," Elwin stammered. "I don't know how it got in."

"He's hallucinating," Barnyard said, nodding to the president. "He's on double medication."

"Aw, don't be so damn stupid Barnyard," Malter chided. "If he's hallucinating, he hears the voices, we don't; and what do you call that thing?" He pointed an accusing finger at Komo. Turning back to Elwin, he nodded a silent order, to which the minder responded by crouching and raising the curtain hem of the bed base.

"Aw boss, there's millions of 'em." He gasped.

"Get them out!" Malter screamed, appalled and angered by this flagrant breach of security. Elwin kicked under the bed, but his leg was caught by Ralph, who twisted the captured limb, forcing the minder to fall flat on his face on the floor. Harvey and Neil rolled from under the bed on the far side, followed by Janet, who clambered out awkwardly and straightened herself up.

"Janet Kennedy!" Malter gasped as he recognized the secretary for small, furry animals.

"Hello Mr. Daisy," Janet replied politely. She was a very well brought-up young lady.

Malter's gaze shifted to Mort and then to Ralph as he emerged from under the bed's end.

"Ms. Kennedy, you've escaped," he said, dryly stating the obvious.

"Yes," she replied, obligingly unsure of whom specifically he thought she had escaped from.

It was then he noticed Harvey and Neil, who was the last to stand up, and flushed by a wave of fear as he recognized the outsider spies, he shouted at Barnyard. "Get security!"

The doctor turned to make a dash for the door but was brought down by a flying leap from Komo that sent him sprawling and winded across the carpet. The furry beast then pounced on Elwin, who was staggering to his feet, and pinned him down by his shoulders while growling menacingly through gnashing teeth. Malter twitched nervously and screamed at Malt, "Who are these people? What are they doing here?"

Malt stared earnestly into his grandson's black eyes.

"These people are my friends," he said.

"Friends!" Malter exploded. "You're the president of the United States; you don't have any friends."

"Malter," Malt said coldly. "I remember you as a boy. You always were a spoiled, self-centered, greedy little brat, just like your father, and you haven't changed a bit in 104 years; you've only gotten worse. You've been pushing me around ever since you revived me, and I'm not going to put up with it anymore. You made me president, and president I am. From now on, I'm writing the scripts."

"Scripts?" Malter said quizzically.

"To start, I'm rewriting that speech tomorrow. Malter, we are not declaring war on South America."

"What?" Malter recoiled, his eyes popping.

"More medication!" Barnyard screamed from the floor.

"Screw your medication," Malt told him. "I haven't even been taking your damn medication."

He reached into the pocket of his nightshirt and cast a handful of pills onto the bed.

"I haven't touched one of those things for weeks," he said triumphantly, and he felt his strength returning as the decision to retake control of his life took hold. "There are going to be some changes around here, I can tell you. For a start, we're going to outlaw cryogenics. From now on, the dead will rest in peace."

Malter began to laugh uncontrollably.

"You old fool," he said. "You think you've avoided your medication. Those pills are nothing but sugar pills. The medication is in the water. You've been having drug-induced delusions. Why don't you just go back to sleep and leave important matters to people who know what they're doing."

"I know what I'm doing. I'm taking over," Malt told his grandson.

Must be a family trait, Neil thought to himself, fearing they were creating something of a Frankenstein's monster. Nevertheless, he was impressed and pleased as Malt went through the motions of taking charge.

Suddenly, Harvey strode to the other side of the bed, and for several seconds, all waited with baited breath to hear what he had to say. He gave a hint of smiling bashfulness, and then he lunged violently at the jug of water on the bedside bureau, pouring half it's contents down his throat with a single gulp and wiping his dribbling mouth with his sleeve.

"Excuse me." He burped. "I needed that."

"Tomorrow," Malt said, "the whole world is going to be told the truth."

"You'll never get away with it," Malter sneered, openly defiant.

Malt looked at his grandson resolutely and said, "Who's going to stop me?"

It was a question Malt asked in perfect innocence, incognizant as he was of the power structure of the regime that had installed him as a puppet.

"I'm on international holovision tomorrow, and the whole world will know."

"Barnyard!" Malter screamed, his frustrations uncontainable. The doctor, as a reflex response, made another attempt on the door. Komo was quick and floored him again with a single leap, but Elwin was quick too. He was up and at Harvey's throat in an instant. The reporter's life was saved by Ralph, who upended the minder and redeposited him on his face.

Malt was on his feet, too, by this stage, jumping up and down on the bed, his stocking feet dancing under his striped nightshirt. Janet screamed, Malt shouted, and Neil ran to assist Harvey, but he was flawed himself as Malter took a wild desperate swing with his fist, and by sheer coincidence—his eyes were closed at the time—clubbed Neil squarely on the jaw.

The room spun, his vision tingled and evaporated like ether on a hot day, and all was suddenly quiet. He felt he was floating in an eternal bliss untill, with a thud, he crashed to the floor and his head imploded with a barrage of strobing lights that flashed passed him and accelerated through a montage of streaming colors. Orange, blue, green, magenta, they fused, blurred then separated and slowly conformed to a pattern, and an image began to take shape. There was a shattered timber structure, dusty air and shreds of colored raffia that floated whimsically in the glare of the midday sun. But as the images of people took form, the colors blurred and the flashing resumed.

The colors separated again and conformed to a new pattern. They were in a holovision studio; Malt was seated before a panel of cameras while Malter, some distance away, oozed into a chair that was carefully guarded by Mort and Ralph. He held an empty jug of water in one hand that hung limply between his legs. Occasionally, he spun the other hand in the air and yelled, "Whoopee!"

The flashing lights took off again, accelerating gracefully with a power and ease that made a Magnobile look like a vintage car. *Tica, tica, tica.* The colors dotted out a coded message. Ghosting images appeared at random and dissolved; sometimes several superimposed themselves at once. He could see his parents, Noel and Nellie. There was a beach and Helen running to meet him, swinging the water from her golden hair. He could see Malter Daisy riding a giant moose through the stars and Mort smiling congenially between his wheezing laugh. The flashing slowed, the colors separated, and again, images composed before him.

Neil was standing, his legs buried to the shin in a pit of black tar. He was surrounded by the peaks of mountains so enormous, the snow glistening in the moonlight from their summits shone as if part of the Milky Way itself. A mountain appeared to be addressing him, "How does, oh piece of nothingness," it seemed to articulate.

"Are you talking to me?" Neil replied, instinctively identifying the tallest mountain as the source of this question.

"You are Neil Hamilton," it said.

"Yes," Neil answered, unsure if this was a question or a statement.

"Do you know who I am?" the voice from the mountain asked, its deep, warm tones shaking the ground untill even Neil's kneecaps rattled.

"Of course I know what you are. You're a mountain. Do you think I can't see that?"

It seemed quite natural to be having a conversation with an igneous protrusion, but Neil was finding his inability to extricate himself from the tar in which he was embedded a frustrating experience.

"I am Peter," the voice told him. "I guard the gates of heaven."

"A damn gatekeeper," Neil mumbled to himself.

"I am an angel. I walk with God," the mountain said. "You are an infinitesimally small, insignificant, perversely mortal piece of nothingness. I have the power to deny you entry into the kingdom of heaven, the power to see, hear and even smell into every part of your soul. I could dissolve you until all that remained was just another greasy molecule in the tar pit. Knowing all this, would you care to explain to me why you deem it fit, in the presence of an angel, to heap profanity on gatekeepers?"

"Ah, er . . ." Neil was not feeling at all comfortable.

"Oh God, how I hate this conversation," the mountain sighed. "We've had it so many times. That's the trouble with these lateral expressions of time. We're all always here forever. Each moment, suspended for eternity. Oh God, I hate it."

"I don't know what you're talking about," the mountain rumbled in perfect unison with Neil.

"You see?" it added. "I knew you were going to say that there, you always do. Why are you always so stupid? You must know it as well as I do by now."

"I don't understand," Neil muttered.

"No, what could a mere mortal possibly know?" the mountain sighed again. "Look, if I've explained it once, I've explained it a billion times. When you die, you stand before the pearly gates. If you want in, you gotta get *authorization* from me."

"I'm dead?" Neil exclaimed, shocked and frightened by the suggestion.

"I'm dead? I'm dead? Can't you think of anything new? Of course you're dead. We're all always dead, forever and ever. Why can't you ask me something intelligent, like, am I still alive?"

"Am I still alive?" Neil and the mountain chimed together.

"Yes, yes, of course you am. God, why do I always say that?" the mountain lamented. "And then I tell you, 'Of course you're still alive.'"

"Alive?" Neil was elated.

"Yes, yes," the mountain grumbled. "We have to endure numerous such encounters before you finally move on to the hereafter. I can see you now. You're arguing with me over the technicalities of what constitutes being alive, but that's twenty years from now."

"Is that when I die?" Neil was quietly terrified and thrilled with a quasi-morbid curiosity at the same time.

"No, that's not when you die. Can't you even remember that?" the mountain roared. "The most important transition since you were born, and you can't even remember?"

"But it hasn't happened yet," Neil said defensively.

"Of course it's happened. It happened 140 years from now when you're guest speaking at the Friends of the Cryogenics Survivors Association. Oh, how I envy you mortals your blissful ignorance, while I have to be aware of every boring second all the time."

Neil didn't know whether he should take the mountain very seriously or not, so he shouted, "Well if I'm not dead yet, what am I doing here?"

"You have to choose," the angel patronized, "don't you? You've come very close to kicking the bucket, to the gates of the kingdom of heaven itself, and now you have the chance to choose between entering the kingdom for eternity or returning to your mortal coil and working through your karma. And we all know what we're going to choose, don't we?"

"I can go back?" Neil and the mountain harmonized. "Yes, send me back. I want to go back."

"That's right, go back," the mountain continued by itself. "I'm here offering you admission to the holy sea of tranquility, the bed of total fulfillment, cosmic center of creation, and the eternal dynamic that encompasses all things that have ever been, that ever will be, that might have been. I'm offering you the ultimate answer to everything, and you want to go back. To *what*!"

The mountain sighed a ripple of vibration that rolled down the cliffs and through the tar pit.

"If you please," Neil requested humbly.

"Oh good, go then," the mountain rumbled, and Neil felt the image fading, leaving him in a fuzzy kind of darkness that filled him from his head to his toes.

Suddenly, he opened his eyes and was temporarily blinded by the glare of lights. As his eyes adjusted, he could see, from his horizontal position, the silhouette of a woman standing by his side.

"Ah, we're awake are we," the voice came from the other side of the bed, and it sounded familiar. Neil rolled his head to the right and looked up. It was Harvey, in the white coat of a medic, his tall gangly body towering like an angelic mountain above him.

"Harvey!" the dazed reporter gasped.

"Horace, Horace Barnard, actually," the doctor corrected as he took Neil by the hand and felt his pulse.

"Where am I?" Neil asked fearfully.

"You're in the Daisylands infirmary," Horace told him. "Best infirmary in the world. Why, we've performed minor dental surgery on the president in this very building."

"Huh?" Neil grunted.

"Oh, darling," the woman to his left leaned down and hugged him. "I knew you'd be all right."

"Helen?" Neil said as he recognized her.

"Stage collapsed on you in the celebrations on Sunday," the doctor informed him. "We almost lost Governor Van Dyke. You're a lucky man. You've been out for three days now. Three more and your medical coverage would have expired."

Neil didn't feel like a lucky man. He just felt giddy, and his head throbbed.

"I wanna go home," he moaned.

"In a few days," Horace advised as Helen looked up hopefully. "He's been badly concussed. We'll keep him under observation, and all being well, you can take him home Friday."

Helen caressed her husband's cheek with the back of her hand.

"Oh my poor dear," she cooed. "What have you been doing to yourself?"

"I don't know, but I promise I'll never do it again," he said.

"I should hope not, you have to get better." Helen bolstered his spirits. "Mr. Impiombartu was on the phone yesterday, and guess what? He said you've got an interview with the president of the United States next month, if you live."

She smiled vigorously but her face paled when Neil's reaction to what she thought was exciting news was less than enthusiastic.

"What!" he shouted, and sat bolt upright in the bed, bringing him into direct eye contact with a picture of Mickey Moose on the far wall.

"I thought you'd be pleased." Helen pouted. "They're going to fly you to Washington especially."

"In a sky plane?" Neil was becoming increasingly alarmed.

Helen and the doctor exchanged glances.

"Well, in an airplane, I expect," she answered him.

"I don't wanna go." Neil struggled to clamber from the bed, but the doctor held him back. "No more interviews; I don't want to see the president. I don't want to see anybody."

He felt weak and fell back helplessly as Helen leaned over him, squeezing his hand reassuringly. The doctor gave a thoughtful grunt and, striding to the medicine cabinet in the corner of the room, withdrew a hypodermic syringe. Neil kept rambling, "No more presidents, and we're going to outlaw moose."

"Neil, Neil," Helen moaned.

"I think we'd better put him on double medication," Horace Barnard said. "It'll keep him calm."

"Oh, my poor darling," Helen repeated as she stroked her delirious husband's face.

"And I've gotta fix the car. Did you see the condition it's in?" Neil rambled on.

The doctor plunged the needle into the raving patient's arm, and his words began to slur. He rested his head on the pillow and sighed with a final exhalation before a contented smile stretched across his face.

"He'll be all right." The doctor comforted the patient's distressed spouse. "He just needs a few days to recover."

"There won't be any long-term damage, will there?" Helen asked anxiously.

"No, not at all. We may have to keep him on medication a while, but there's no reason to believe he won't make a complete recovery. Even if he didn't, we could always put him on ice till we knew what to do. I could explain it to you over dinner if you like? Are you doing anything this evening?"

He smiled hospitably.

"Why that would be lovely. Yes, thank you," she acquiesced.

Neil mumbled. "No dad. Not another circus." Then he promptly vomited into the mattress.

"Nurse!" Doctor Barnard screamed. "Nurse!"

A young nurse with a plain but kind face appeared at the door of the wardroom.

"Clean him up and change his drip, I've got other patients to attend to," the doctor ordered before turning to Helen.

"Shall we go?" he said, gesturing to the door, and as they disappeared, Neil closed his eyes and let his mind go. He could hear voices calling him, and he felt a dull throb in his head. Suddenly Mort's head was hovering over him, staring down through his baggy black circles.

"His eyes are open," the underworlder droned. "He's back." And there were cheers.

Neil sat up quickly, Janet and Harvey were beside him, breathing sighs of relief, and Komo was licking his feet. Neil saw them all watching.

"Quick," he shouted, "somebody hit me."

"We wouldn't do dat," Ralph said genuinely.

"I would."

"Harvey!" Janet reprimanded him.

Neil tried punching himself in the head but was effectively restrained. They hadn't told him yet, but he had to get well, holding as he did an important new government position. Neil's appointment to the Federal Bureau of Utter Nonsense meant his old life on the outside may have been over, but his life as an insider was just beginning.

Printed in the United States
By Bookmasters